I0654998

Frederic Ashby

The rural epic: Willie and Alice

A tale in rhyme

Frederic Ashby

The rural epic: Willie and Alice
A tale in rhyme

ISBN/EAN: 9783337175641

Printed in Europe, USA, Canada, Australia, Japan

Cover: Foto ©Andreas Hilbeck / pixelio.de

More available books at **www.hansebooks.com**

THE RURAL EPIC;

OR,

WILLIE AND ALICE.

A TALE IN RHYME.

BY F. W. ASHBY, M. D.,

A Member of the Fiftieth Indiana Legislature.

MOTTO: "Some noted course I'll strive to run;
'I must aim high to hit the sun.'"

—Page 11.

INDIANAPOLIS:

SENTINEL COMPANY, PRINTERS AND BINDERS.

1877.

TO

PREFACE.

THIS little work is the result of the leisure moments intervening between the business hours of the author.

It, however, like all other human productions, shows upon its face many imperfections. It was written for the friends of the author and not for the critic, for in "his eyes even the heavens themselves are impure."

Much has been said and written about original ideas, but a little thought will convince the unbiased mind that such an idea does not, nor never did, exist, except in the mind of Deity.

For example, who could have invented the word "steamboat," or "telegram" before the age of steam or telegraph? Man originates nothing. What he calls invention is the result of hint or accident.

The author is therefore free to admit that he has availed himself of facts and fancies from every accessible source, but gives credit to the authors who have aided him in his task, such as Shakspeare, Burns, Scott, Pollok, Young, Thompson, Hogg, and others.

The scene reaches back forty or fifty years, to a period when the manners of our people were much plainer than now, and for this reason the book bears the title of "Rural Epic," and hence, also, the principal characters are known by the unpoetic names of Green and Brown.

The intention is to inspire the young with a desire to strive for greatness and goodness; to prove that we must not do "evil that good may come," and that we should trust in God.

The accomplishment of these ends, or any one of them, will afford great satisfaction to the

AUTHOR.

EUREKA, SPENCER CO., IND.,
        January 8, 1877.

INTRODUCTION.

Come, gentle reader, sail with me
In Fancy's ship o'er Fiction's sea,
To fair Utopia's floral clime,
Where dreamers dwell and poets rhyme.

Our anchor's weighed, the ship's in trim;
No clouds the sky of thought bedim;
Our baggage ready, sails unfurled,
We leave this busy, care-worn world.

How fast our native shores recede,
As on we sail at sunbeam speed;
Now nought is left for us to view
Save one small line of smoky blue.
The splashing spray before our prow,
Rolls up like soil before the plow;
Or like the snow, when whirl'd before
December's stern and wintry roar.
How swiftly drives our heaving sail
Before Imagination's gale,
With swelling canvas wide unfurl'd
Like some huge bird from foreign world.

Above we image, yet untold,
A sky of pure and burnished gold,

Where meteor fancies star-like run,
More brilliant than the dazzling sun;
Or cast the eye below with me
Adown the depths of Fiction's sea,
And feast the soul on that bright prize
So near akin to Paradise.
Here thought on thought, in mazes whirl'd,
Goes giddying 'round this glowing world
Like flash on flash of lightning red,
At twilight calm, above the head.

Now look beyond; we meet the whiles
Of Peace and Joy—those witching isles—
And contrawise, are forced to see
The damning rocks of Misery;
And farther on, behold! behold!
A glowing line of glittering gold—
The ravished eye is forced to yield;
It is Utopia's nearing field.

"Breakers ahead!"—for land is near—
"Breakers ahead!"—the echoes hear.
Our anchor now lies in the sand,
We'll view, at will, the Elysian strand.

THE RURAL EPIC;

OR,

WILLIE AND ALICE.

THE HIGH RESOLVE.

Bright Phœbus, with a sleepy eye,
Was sinking in the western sky,
And as he left us for the night,
With magic pencil dipt in light,
He eastward drew a glorious bow,
Which made ten thousand beauties flow
From what, but, now was threat'ning cloud
Enmantling earth so like a shroud.
And as the sky grew more serene,
More variegated was the scene;
Here, mountain-like, piled one on one.
Rich golden clouds above the sun,
And there, again, were to be seen
Fantastic shapes of silver sheen,
Sailing like ships fast through the sky,
Delighting well wild Fancy's eye.

But further they, and faster, run
As lower sinks the setting sun,
And fainter and yet fainter grew
Those golden beauties to the view
Of him whose eyes were upward turn'd
Where late such glowing pictures burn'd.
At length the sun low in the west,
Sank slowly down, as if to rest,
While here and there some random ray,
Bright beaming from the god of day,
Would strike, perchance, some village spire,
And change it into living fire;
Or tip with red some lofty tree,
Whose head high tower'd o'er hill and lea.
Then shut at last his dazzling eye,
But left behind a blushing sky,
Which soon resum'd its natural hue
Of pure, ethereal, lovely blue;
And while the "sable goddess," Night,
Shut out from earth this world of light,
The whippowil, in plaintive lay,
Fit requiem sang of dying day.

The whilst the stars too, one by one,
Repaying earth for loss of sun,
Appeared, with twinkling diamond eyes,
High hanging in the upper skies,
Till Heaven's vast space seem'd dotted o'er,
A sea of fire without a shore;
And, while each, seemingly would try,
The other's splendor to outvie,

Pale Luna, like a stately queen,
Uprising in the east was seen:
And, like high lady o'er peasant dame,
Soon paled the glittering host with shame,
And made them quickly, star by star,
Retire within the heavens afar,
Till but a few (the bolder ones),
Remained and shown like little suns,
And made the moon a glorious train
As march'd she o'er blue ether's plane.

On such an eve might have been seen
The model form of Willie Green,
(Whom we shall make, unless we fail,
The worthy hero of our tale),
Low sitting in his cottage door,
Where oft at night he'd pondered o'er
The pains and pleasures of his life,
Its joys and sorrows, fears and strife,
When he his work had neatly done,
And all his mother's errands run.
And as he sat thus pensively,
And gazed upon the scene which we
Have tried (but very vainly tried),
To image, as by nature dyed,
In studious mood, low mutter'd he
The following soliloquy:

" Yon heavenly panoramic scene
  Fit emblem is of life, I ween;
  The frowning cloud that thundered by,
  Painting destruction on the sky,

And show'ring down its hail and rain
As past it drove o'er hill and plain,
Well represents life's ills and toils,
Its dangers, threat'nings and turmoils,
Its sorrows, and its bitter tears,
Its adverse winds and chilling fears.
But on this cloud a bow was bent,
Which to the earth its beauties lent.

"And so it is when storms arise
And drive athwart our *mental* skies,
Some bow of promise soon appears
To quiet and remove our fears;
Nor seldom rises cloud so dark
But what some scintillating spark
Of hope, or promised bow of peace,
Springs up to bid our troubles cease.

"Thus far hath been my life, to me,
A stormy cloud, a raging sea;
God grant that yet some cheering ray
Of sunshine may light up my way,
And warm, ere long, with gladsome joy
The heart of this poor cottage boy!
Oh! what were life without a sun
Of hope to light our path, as run
We, courser-like, at random o'er
The hills and dales of Time's rough shore.

"Those phantom clouds which float me by,
Like islands in the azure sky,

Do represent to my crude mind
The various struggles of mankind
For wealth, for honor, and for place
So highly prized by Adam's race.
Some loaded are with silver bright,
And some there seem as black as night,
While some again of gold appear,
And move them in a stately sphere;
Some higher float, and some more low,
Some swiftly fly, and some move slow;
Now in these varied clouds, I ween,
The sev'ral grades of men are seen.
Since man was born for purpose high,
Since 'Hope's enchantments never die,'
I'll nerve me like a hero bold,
And strive my mental man to mold
For greatness; and I'll carve my name
Upon the highest hight of fame:
Some noted course I'll strive to run;
I must 'aim high to hit the sun.'

"I love 'my country, and my kind,'
And love of these inspires my mind
To strike for some immortal plan
To benefit my fellow-man.
And love I, too, with heart sincere,
A maiden sweet, to me most dear;
And she, my guardian angel bright,
Shall nerve my mind by day and night
For high resolve, for honor, fame,
For wealth, for an undying name."

WILLIE'S HOME AND MOTHER.

Hard by Ohio's classic stream
Began our hero's mind to gleam;
Began his youthful soul to fire
With hot ambition's strong desire.
'Twas here upon some rising ground,
(The remnant of an Indian mound),
There stood a cottage neat and clean.
Where lived his mother Minnie Green—
A lady she, of noble mind:
Such pleasant mein, a heart so kind;
Such modest manner and address
Did Lady Green always possess.
That none e'er saw her but inferred
She "was not of the common herd."

Her graces fine would well command
Profound respect in any land.
From kindred, now, and friends away
"Yet she had known a better day."
Her husband dear to her, and kind,
Of fortune good, and giant mind.
Was doomed to quit this world of strife
Ere he had seen the noon of life,

And find, in youth. an early grave,
And leave his bosom friend a slave
To woe's keen pangs on life's cold stage,
Where storms of sorrow ever rage;
Yet she had left one earthly joy,
Her precious Willie, orphan boy.
But scarce had rolled six years away
And emptied them in Time's great bay,
Ere Want with all his train had come,
And bade her seek an humbler home.
Though left with means to live at ease,
And ferry o'er life's stormy seas,
Misfortunes followed one by one,
And duty to her noble son,
Compelled her, in this pressing strait,
To leave New York, her native state.

"How hard to be of friends bereft;
To be a poor. lone widow left;
Exiled from kindred and from home,
A stranger in strange lands to roam!"
Exclaimed this lady, while "farewell!"
In tender accents. marked the swell,
The ebbs and flows of bosoms kind
She soon for aye must leave behind.
"And must I bid," she said. "adieu
To New York City, where I drew
My earliest and my sweetest breath,
And where I hoped to live till death?
'Tis even so; then let me hie
From fatherland to live and die!"

With her scant purse, now all her wealth,
Except her boy, and books and health,
Her high resolves, and her good name,
Unto the western world she came,
Where, we have said, a cot she found
Upon Ohio's fertile ground.
This cot stood on a small domain,
Diversified with hill and plain,
Which, ere she left her native town,
She purchased of old Major Brown,
Who by long years of toil and care
Had made himself a millionaire.

On Willie here her means and time
She spent; nor thought it any crime
To stint the body for the mind
So much her inmost soul inclined
This tender, plastic bud to see
Grow up a tow'ring, lofty tree;
To see him scale the mount Renown,
And from its highest peak look down
Upon the plodding world below
(All anxious then his trump to blow,
And make his praise like geysers rise
In spouting volleys to the skies),
Was now her only living theme;
Her thought each day, each night her dream,
To see her son (O! glorious sight!),
Tread at his ease this dizzy hight,
Where reels and turns the common brain,
If e'er it looks adown the plain,

Would well reward the toil she thought
A mother's zeal and care had wrought.
Quoth she: "There ne'er was mental field
That promised such a golden yield."—

Methinks there's more than fancy here,
Or fiction. Search o'er nature's sphere—
Lives there the mother on time's shore
Who has not painted o'er and o'er,
With pencil dipt in fancy wild,
Some golden future for her child?

WILLIE.

Mayhap 't would please the reader's ear,
Somewhat of Willie now to hear.
Come, list ye then, how he beguiled
His precious moments, yet a child.
His constant habit was to pore
For hours each day, o'er books of lore,
And ere eight winters fled could speak
The German, Latin, French and Greek,
And ere his ninth returning spring
The greatest poets well could sing;
And at the early age of ten
Could wield a philosophic pen;
The starry worlds with ease could trace
And mark their course through boundless
    space;
And to his great Newtonian brain
The deepest problems all were plain;
And e'er the nineteenth time he'd seen
The leaves in autumn lose their green,
His mighty mind with ease could soar
In boundless flights, all sciences o'er;
Through all her boundless fields could roam
And ever seem to be at home.
And yet withal, so modest he,
That gained he no celebrity

Beyond his few unletter'd friends,
Whose praises no great fame attends,
For who'd suppose a cot to hold
Such mental gems, worth more than gold?

But we can not minutely say
How passed his early life away,
For golden time like lightning flies—
A moment born, that instant dies.
Then stop we not at length to tell
What various things his youth befell,
How, fast before him up and down,
The hoop roll'd o'er his native town:
Or how, at marble, top, or ball,
He far excelled his fellows all;
How all his classmates he surpassed,
So kindly did he learn, and fast;
Tell how his teacher he obeyed,
How truth did all his thoughts pervade,
And might we too, had we but time,
Employ some stanzas of our rhyme,
In telling o'er his rural feats,
When far removed from crowded streets;
Tell how, at his new western home,
He loved the woods and fields to roam;
And how much studious pains he took
To comprehend vast nature's book:
At ev'ry step, and ev'ry turn,
His mind with some new thought would burn,
And view'd he man, or mite, or clod,
He looked through nature up to God.

2

Might tell how seated at the brook
With rod and line and baited hook,
He could, with true Waltonian art,
Do honor to the angler's part;
How he could wind the hunter's horn,
And chase the fox from morn to morn;
And how, with modern gunner's skill,
The wary quail on wing could kill;
Tell how, inured to rugged toil,
His careful hand could till the soil.
How four long years, while yet a boy,
Old Major Brown gave him employ,
Sometimes as his cashier and clerk,
Sometimes at some more slavish work.
Sometimes it was his pleasing task
In Alice Brown's sweet smiles to bask,
While she her plastic mind would store
With Willie's rich and varied lore.
She and her brother spent their time
In wand'ring o'er the fields sublime
Of varied science, side by side,
With manly Willie as their guide.
These traits and acts, with many more,
Which we've omitted by the score,
'T would give us pleasure to rehearse
At length in our imperfect verse,
But said we that we could not tell
"What various things his youth befell,"
So with these hasty hints we pass,
(For constant runs Time's hour-glass.)

The dial's shadow constant moves,
As man's perception clearly proves,
Though moving it was never seen,
By mortal eye, since time hath been,
Yet observation serves to show
That it is moving, howe'er slow,—
So passes childhood's early stage
From infancy to youth's full age.
We look us round, as 't were to-day,
And see a helpless infant lay
Upon its mother's dandling knee,
A tiny angel, sinless; free
From all the mental storms that rage
Through the excited brain of age;
But look to-morrow, you behold
That infant then a giant bold,
Perhaps devising some great plan
For forcing from his fellow-man
Such praise by his superior nod
As should be due to none but God;
Or else, with war's red flag unfur'd,
Strikes terror through a trembling world.
But yest'ren, on his mother's lap
Our hero wore his baby cap:
The change, since he an infant lay,
Seems but the work of one poor day;
Seems as some fairy's magic wand,
Alone, by some unknown command,
Could modify great nature's plan
And turn a babe so soon to man.

But howsoe'er this all may seem;
Be it reality or dream,
We know 't is but a step, a breath,
E'en from the cradle down to death.
We said: "ere eighteen falls had fled
And dropped their leaves on Willie's head,
His mighty mind with ease could soar
In boundless flights all science o'er,"
And now we find him just nineteen,
Of form as fine as e'er was seen.
His forehead was of classic mold,
Symmetrical, projecting, bold,
And arching, dome-like, full and high,
In grandeur o'er his noble eye;
While 'round his head such tresses flow
As rival well the glossy crow,
Embellishing his caput fine,
And winding 'round his brow benign,
Resembling, in its vine-like curl,
The eglantine's poetic twirl;
And as the sun lights up the sky
So lights his face his brilliant eye,
As it beneath his brow doth roll,
A perfect mirror of his soul;
For as the sun its light doth beam
So from his eye each thought doth gleam.
Well marked his features were, and strong,
Well formed his Roman nose, though long;
His graceful cheeks, though strong and high
Well suited were to his fine eye,

And in his mouth, and chin, and face
Like manly beauties, too, we trace.
By absence long from crowded town
His skin was slightly tinged with brown,
Yet, like the ocean's ebb and flow,
Still could the color come and go—
Aye, quick his cheek with red could fire,
If blushed by love, or roused by ire.
His model neck and manly chest
Would far surpass the sculptor's best;
And ne'er was known in any land
More tapered limb or perfect hand.
A finer form ne'er hath been seen
Than was the form of Willie Green,
Surpassing far in ev'ry part
The greatest sculptor's noble art.—

Methinks some gentle lady's mind
Mayhap is ill at ease to find
Such noble mind should ever grace
The features of so coarse a face—
But list ye, at the ocean's roar,
And mark the roughness of the shore,
Or note the mild and harmless dove,
As gentle as her song of love.
Then go, the world minutely scan,
You'll find strong features mark the man
Of gen'rous, high and noble mind;
Of firmness great, and bosom kind;
And contrawise we also see
That features of less mark'd degree

But serve to note the empty shells
Where utter nothing oftimes dwells.—
From further comment we refrain
And turn us to our tale again.
In Willie's gen'rous breast we find
A nature noble as his mind;
His heart was pictured on his face;
Each thought, with ease, we here might
        trace;
So frank, so honest, was the youth
"That thought was speech, and speech was
        truth."

Few maidens 'scape bold Cupid's darts
Within the sphere of such warm hearts.
We need not tarry here to prove
His but another name for love;
Yet heated by no fickle flame,
That burnt what e'er in reach it came;
It flashed no sudden powder blaze,
No lightning gleam, then scarce a haze;
But burnt one steady, warming flame,
Which naught but death had power to tame.

It had one altar, was one fire,
And that not kindled to expire.
It worshipped at one shrine alone;
Loved one fair maid, loved Alice Brown,
Than whom, a lovlier maiden true,
Ne'er gazed upon the heavens blue.

ALICE.

Reared far from the deceitful smile,
('So practiced oft in courtly style')
Her heart was free from artful guile.
Aye, nature's own true child was she,
With soul of pure simplicity.
She little of deception dreamed;
All things to her were what they seemed;
Yet were her manner and her mind
By classic tutors well refined;
And oft she had the company
Of noted guests of high degree,
And all who saw her truly swore
Such beauty was ne'er seen before.

Her soft, bewitching, lovely eyes
Seemed borrowed lustre from the skies.
Her auburn ringlets waving rolled
In graceful curls like burnished gold,
Nor did such tresses ever grace
The features of a lovlier face;
Her cheeks were like the blushing rose;
Description fails to paint her nose.
Fair as the driven snow her skin,
Beyond compare her dimpled chin;
"Her lips were lovlier far to see
Than the ripe cherry from the tree,

And richer far their juice to taste
Than e'er was from the cherry pressed."
Her neck was neck of graceful swan,
No limner has a finer drawn.
Her ebbing, flowing bosom, too,
Encasing her own heart so true,
Scarce peeping o'er silken gown
When e'er a deeper sigh was drawn,
Would cause in fitful streams to start
Love's passion from the coldest heart.
Her well-turned limbs and queenly form
Ten thousand hearts could take by storm,
And the sweet music of her words
Struck on the ear like silver chords
Of golden harp, when o'er them strays
The hand with which an angel plays;
For music gushed from her pure soul
Like water from a broken bowl.
Nor did more graceful, stately tread
E'er dash the dew from flow'rets head.

The lads and lassies far away,
All common practice made to say:
"As beautiful as Alice Brown,"
So famous had her graces grown.

Why wonder then that Willie's heart,
Received love's spear and felt its smart;
A greater wonder far would be
How from such influence he could flee.
Nor need we say in metric words,
That Alice, too, felt love's sweet cords;

For nature's laws are so designed,
That like to like is e'er inclined.
True as the needle to the pole,
And constant as the brooklet's roll
When winding the green hills between,
Was Alice Brown to Willie Green—
More loving couple ne'er was seen.
The world to them was fair and bright,
All perfect day, no shade of night;
For them all nature wore a charm
That made them feel secure from harm,
From them each thought not fit for heaven
By love's impulsive tide was driven.—

But ah! how false youth's golden dream!
We wake; few things are what they seem.
O! could we all the future know!
We oft, to 'scape a world of woe,
Might snap the brittle thread of life,
And free us from the coming strife.
But God, in his most wond'rous plan
For governing his creature, man,
Has drawn a darksome veil to screen,
What is to come from what has been.

The harmless lambkin skips and plays
A moment e'er the butcher slays,
And oft we feel the greatest glee
When verging on deep trouble's sea.—

THE PROMENADE.

Whilst winding o'er a flow'ry vale,
Each hearing, telling, love's soft tale,
Or halting now for some choice flower;
Now viewing the rich landscape o'er,
They sought at length the cooler shade
Where Willie to fair Alice said:
"Thy brother Allen we've not seen
For three long years, my lovely queen,
Nor hath he cheered his anxious home,
From Russia, England, France, or Rome,
By letter, which he oft should give,
To tell us that he yet doth live.
His mind, perchance, he's wont to store
With ancient Grecian, Roman lore,
Where learning's fountain was of yore;
Or else, perchance, some soft amour
Hath thus prolonged his eastern tour.
Or rather yet, the scenery grand,
So richly sung in ev'ry land,
Mayhap hath wandered him away,
And made him lengthen out his stay.
But why let Rome's rich, classic sky,
So charm his soul, and please his eye?
Why worship at a Grecian shrine,
Or bow before the crags of Rhine?

Or sue for foreign lady's hand,
When beauty blooms in his own land?
Doth not the charming sky of Rome
O'erhang our country, and our home?
And England's silver haze is seen
High roofing o'er our mountains green.

"Oh! dry thy tears, my lovely maid!
Ah! woe is me for what I've said!
O! dry thy tears, I still will be
A friend and brother unto thee!
For by the powers of heaven above
My love for thee shall constant prove.
Thine eyes of soft, ethereal blue,
Are like rich flow'rets set with dew,
But dry them now, it grieves me sore
To see such torrents from them pour.
I fain would show a diamond ring,
(But it would make new fountains spring),
And other gifts from him I hold,
More worth to me than Ophir's gold—
But come, divert thy troubled mind
With thoughts of some more soothing kind.
Come, dry the teardrops from thine eyes,
And view beneath the soft spring skies
Ohio's glories as they spread
Around, above, beneath thy head.
Like mellow cadence of sweet song,
So purls this dulcet stream along,
And ev'ry bough, and ev'ry spray
Beats time to her aquatic lay;

While join, in chorus, the sweet notes
Made by ten thousand warbler's throats;
And dance the trees on either shore
To the sweet music of her roar;
And o'er her rugged hills the while
On this grand scene look down and smile,
And as young infants sleeping lie,
When hushed by some sweet lullaby,
So, on her'gently heaving breast
Her children, the rich *islands* rest.
Yet sad are Nature's songs to me
When in thine eyes such floods I see."

Here Alice sighed and shook her head,
But filled with grief, no word she said—

"And richer, far, one smile from thee
Than all the islands in the sea.
See, dressed in robes of living green,
Sweet Nature sits a very queen.
Her daughter, Spring, rejoiced to see
Stern Winter from earth's borders flee,
Has richly spread. with magic hand,
Her richest carpets o'er the land;
Around us, too, Spring's waiting-maid
Chaste Flora, has her offering laid,
Has shed, in rich, profusive show'rs,
Her ever varying store of flowers,
And wreathed these hills and decked yon
        lawn
As 't were to feed Thought's fancy on.

"Here peep the modest flow'rets through
The morning's crystal, balmy dew,
As peep thy lovely eyes through tears
Excited by foreboding fears.

"Here bows the grass's tiny head,
To ev'ry gentle breeze's tread,
And there the violet's modest hue,
Resembling heaven's own lovely blue,
Adds, by soft contrast with the green,
Fresh life and beauty to the scene;
And here, like our fond hearts, do twine
The ivy and the eglantine.—
Oh! now thy smiles light up thy tears
Like rainbows when the sun appears—
Here buttercups, and daisies too,
Each morning drink the sparkling dew,
And here the roses ruddy lips
The same pure nectar sweetly sips.

"See you rich fields of waving grains,
Where golden-sceptered Ceres reigns,
And the green forest's ev'ry spray
Dressed in its richest spring array—
Yet all were sad to me and sere,
Without thy presence, Alice dear.

"There stretches out a level lawn,
Complete as by some limner drawn,
With here and there and ancient mound,
Which like small mountains dot the ground;

Or like small islets to be seen
Upon this sea of living green:
While far around the blue hills rise,
Chain beyond chain of varying size,
And skyward point their flinty spires,
(Reflecting, steel-like, Sol's bright fires),
And saying, with one sweet accord,
'We own thee our creator, Lord.'
And while their spires are upward turned,
And with the sun's hot rays are burned,
Ohio bathes and cools their feet,
And daily does the task repeat,
And spreads her placid bosom free,
A mirror bright, themselves to see.
Midway within this Paradise,
See stately palace buildings rise,
Whose snow-white walls far on yon lea
Remind us of some sail at sea;
Fit lodging for a titled lord
Those gorgeous dwellings would afford.
Betwixt us and that Eden, too,
A lowly cot, we scarce can view,
Like some small cloud 'twixt us and heaven,
By adverse winds at random driven.
In this, the lowly, humble cot,
I, with my mother, share my lot;
In that, remote from tower and town,
Besides thy father, Major Brown.
Upon my word, I do declare,
Was never scene so passing fair
As manor of this millionaire;

But since the name of "*Eden's*" given
To that grand place, so like a heaven,
It still with heaven would ill compare
Without thee, Alice, angel fair—
Whose face illumes thy father's walls
As chandeliers do princely halls:
This scene is fair, and very fair,
Yet it with thee will not compare."

With blush and smile, and head awry,
Young Alice passed these praises by;
Yet felt, perchance, that they were due,
For ev'ry word he said was true.
He dealt not in vile flattery,
His heart was true sincerity.
Then pressed by Willie to declare,
If love for him her bosom bear—
(Though whom she loved he knew before,
For oft they'd told their wooings o'er),
With modest mien, and face aside,
"She half consenting, half denied;"
Then with her rich, melodious voice
She named the object of her choice—

"My own true Willie, without thee
That palace would a prison be,
And that sweet cot with thy rich love
I'd scarce exchange for heaven above.
With thee—but hark! what clattering sound
Comes echoing from the hills around?
It seems the sound of charging steeds
When battles rage and bravery bleeds!"

THE ARREST.

They looked, and lo! ten armed men
Came, spurring steeds o'er glade and glen,
Like robbers, of a savage band,
When plundering in an outlaw'd land;
But check the riders now the rein
And slowly wind them o'er the plain,
Then halting in a skirt of wood,
The band before the lovers stood,
When one, out-stepping from the rest,
In voice official, Green addressed:—

"Sir, list, thou murd'rous villian! heed!
While I thy body-process read!"—
His eyes, like lightning in a storm,
Soon flashed them o'er the legal form—
"The commonwealth, by stern command,
Doth seize thee with its iron hand,
Doth bid me drag thee to its bar,
Where Justice shall thy doom declare.
Report is rife in all the land
That thou dost wield a bloody hand.
Suspicion too, is roused to tell
That thou hast done a deed of hell,
And circumstance of late is known
Which says you've murdered Allen Brown.

Come, mount this steed, thou wicked Cain,
Or by the pow'r of this, my train,
Sharp force shall hie thee o'er the plain!"

"O, heaven protect us!" Alice said,
" And is my only brother dead?"
 As on her bosom dropp'd her head,
 Like faded rose, in autumn's frost,
 When its rich tint of summer's lost;
 Then reeling sank, like dying dove,
 Or blighted hope o'er buried love.—

" By heavens!"—his eyes were flashing fire
 And burning was his soul with ire;
 Red rage was gleaming in his face;
 The trembling clan drew back apace.—
" By heavens!" the madden'd Willie cries,
"Suspicion's head is full of eyes;
 Report's foul tongue most foully lies;
 Nor circumstance is there to prove
 I've slain the friend whom most I love,
 And woe to him, of this vile squad,
 Who first lays hands, so help me God!
 'T is true that Fate, beyond control,
 With poverty hath cursed my soul,
 Yet honor's flame through it doth roll.
 I would not stain my heart with crime
 For all earth's gold and pomp sublime;
 And should I stoop to deed so fell
 Then seek my soul the lowest hell!

Palsied my frame, be still my breath
For aye!   Before dishonor death!—
See, ruffians, what your work hath done!
The fairest flower beneath the sun
Lies panting here, and deadly pale,
O'ercome by your infernal tale.
Go, bear her to her mother's arms,
And bid her quell those false alarms.—
I see her father 'mong you stands,
As Satan did in Eden's lands,
Tempting to sin as pure a pair
As ate forbidden fruit when there.
" And 't were for his daughter's sake,
And his gray hairs, his head should ache."
Full well knows he his son's not dead,
And knows no curse rests on my head.
He wishes but to curb my pride
And drive me from his daughter's side;
As well might Satan, by false love,
Attempt to lure from heaven above
A saint, in all its glory there,
As drive me from my Alice fair;
As snap the cords which make us one—
No pow'r can do 't beneath the sun."

His passion calmed, quoth he: " In brief,
Why come as 't were against a thief?
Why bring a troop of armed men
And hunt me down o'er hill and glen?
Dost fear the lion in his den?—

With stainless soul, and conscience clear,
The honest man hath naught to fear.
No ghostly visions haunt his brain,
Of virtue robbed, or fellow slain;
He fears not e'en an armed train.
His conscience is a bulwark strong.
'Thrice armed is he,' when free from wrong—
Vile Slander's blasting my good name;
My honor lost, I must reclaim.
Come weal, come woe! whate'er betide,
I'll mount the steed and with thee ride."—

They're gone, and silence nature shrouds,
Like calm succeeding stormy clouds;
They're gone, and the ensuing calm
Renews the soul like soothing balm;
But time alone can heal the wound
That in fair Alice' heart is found;
Restore the rose-tint to her cheek
And fire again her spirits bleak;
Or Willie Green to her restore,
And then she's Alice Brown once more.

On couch of sorrow now she lies
With heated brain and streaming eyes;
Now Reason staggers, mocks, and reels
As one when too much wine he feels—
"Who's there? who's there? speak, fiend,"
        she cries
"With glittering dagger, ha, he flies!

What darksome forms dance me before,
With eyes of fire, and hands of gore!
It is the fiends of hell I see—
Avaunt! avaunt! ye spectres flee!
Or bring my brother back to me!"—
They're gone, but a succeeding train
Comes thundering on—"my brain, my brain!
O, Willie!" mark! she rears her head;
Ah! back she falls, she swoons as dead!

THE PRISON.

On wheels of Time months rolled away,
Yet Willie still in prison lay;
His mind, like some strong beast of prey,
Devoured such food as it could find,
And he was to his fate resigned.
Day after day he journeyed o'er
The fertile fields of legal lore,
Till, in his mighty mind were blent
The stores of Greenleaf, Chitty, Kent;
Till Blackstone's thoughts were all his own
With num'rous authors now unknown.

His mother now bowed down with grief,
Could find no comfort or relief.
Deep sorrow's waves did constant roll,
Like ocean's billows, through her soul—
"Where now the golden hopes," quoth she,
"I, in the future, once could see,
The sunny future, once so bright.
Is now, to me, a darksome night,
For now, alas! My only son,
His course of life hath nearly run.
He might have carved on Fame's bright sky,
His name, in golden letters high,
But now, dishonored, he must die!

O! cruel Fate! my source of joy,
Thou art determined to destroy!
The staff of my declining years
Thou't take, and leave me but my tears."

Not so with Brown, the millionaire;
No trouble drove him to despair.
With purse-proud soul and heart of steel,
No drop of pity could he feel
For Willie, or his daughter fair;
Buoyant, his spirits seemed as air;
But yet, like lion in his lair,
Revenge sat couched to make his spring,
And poison with his mortal sting.
"By pow'r supreme!'" the old man said.
"This driv'ling whiffler's peering head
Shall seek his level! Then, by Jove!
His level found, there let him love!
There let him sue, in lower spheres,
For maiden's hand among his peers.
Bright Sol may hide his shining face,
Pale Luna cease her rounds to trace;
May fall the stars, like streams of fire,
Till worlds unnumber'd all expire,
But Alice Brown shall ne'er be seen
The spouse of such as Willie Green."

THE DREAM.

PART I.

We turn to Alice, now, and find
Her clothed again in her right mind;
But lily pale her faded cheek,
As humble nun, in convent meek.
For four long weeks, on bed of pain,
With fev'rish limbs and racking brain
She lay;   Nor Hygia wished to see:
Cared but from future woe to flee.
'T was while afflicted, thus she lay,
A vision strange had she one day.
She took Aurora's wings of light
And flew to deepest depths of night.
So light, so airy was her form,
She flew like lightning in a storm.
She looked adown the closing track,
Her weeping friends all beck her back.
"She saw below her, fair unfurl'd,
One-half of all the glowing world,
Where oceans rolled, and rivers ran,
To bound the aims of sinful man;"
Yet, quick as thought, she left behind
The less'ning earth and sporting wind;
As on, and on, and on she flew
The trackless fields of ether through.

A boundless sea, without a shore,
Vast space spreads out her mind before.
But still as fast she parts the skies
New worlds on worlds successive rise,
And quicker than by fancy drawn,
They come, are seen; They go, are gone.
As quickly came, as quickly passed,
Succeeding worlds as did the last,
For all, (so fast she traveled on),
Were moment seen and moment gone.
Yet on, and on, and on she flew
The trackless fields of ether through,
Till in her flight rose up a shore
All full of bones and streams of gore,
Resembling naught she'd seen before.
But tired with her weary flight,
She stopped to rest her wings of light;
First poising high awhile she stood
And gazed upon the scene of blood;
Then slowly sailing three times 'round
She softly lit upon the ground.
Great piles of bones heaped mountain high,
Whose summits seemed to prop the sky,
Stood in unnumbered heaps around
While blood in torrents drenched the ground,
And swiftly swept o'er hill and plain
As water sweepeth after rain.
While gazing thus in gloomy mood
Two giant forms before her stood.
Their height was sixty feet or more;
A scythe one on his shoulder bore.

The other held in his huge hand
A busy glass of running sand.
This said, in voice like lion's roar,
"You've sought, young maid, a friendless
        shore.
If you but tarry in this land,
Till through this glass shall run this sand,
My friend shall with his scythe destroy
Your life, with ev'ry hope and joy:
Your warm, impulsive, youthful blood
Shall help to swell yon gory flood.
Your bones shall bleach beneath the sky
On yon ossific mountain high."

Thus saying with his giant hand
He roughly shook the glass of sand,
Then looked at Alice, then his friend,
As if to say: "Do what you intend."

That raised his scythe, as if to say:
"This moment you shall pass away."—
Young Alice did not think to fly,
But turned her head away to die.
A moment gone, she turned again;
She was alone upon the plain:
Or when, or how the monsters fled
She could not tell to save her head.
She hears a dreadful thunder sound,
And turns herself again around—
Two clouds of giants black the ground.
With sword, and spear, and helmet bright
They seemed prepared for dreadful fight,

Their forms were like the forest oak,
Like roaring storm their voices broke.
The hideous noises which they rang,
Of slang, and bang and battle clang,
All sounded such infernal din,
She put her ears her fingers in.
Their helmets bright, outshone the sun,
They wielded swords would weigh a ton.
Their spears were beams from trunks of
        trees,
Which they could thrust with perfect ease.
The leaders on great war steeds prance;
The armies stop, and now advance;
They circle, wheel, and then retreat,
As if they dreaded, each, defeat.
Again they turn, again advance,
And poise on high the deadly lance.
Once more they circle, wheel, retire;
Each waiting on the other's fire;
Then rush, like wrath, the giant foes,
And in the mortal combat close.

But when they clashed in deadly fight,
She could not bear the dreadful sight.
On flitting pinions, wide outspread,
She quick resum'd her airy tread,
And on, and on, and on she flew,
The trackless fields of ether through,
And flying thus, far off, she spies
The glowing fields of Paradise;
With might and main to reach them tries.

But vain her effort; fast they wind,
In space unmeasured, far behind.
The more her wings, for glory spread,
The farther from the place she fled.
At length her wings of light wax small;
She feels that she, ere long, must fall.
She sees the bounds of darkness rise
Like black despair before her eyes.
Yet on, and on, and on she flew,
The trackless fields of darkness through.
But when she reached the realms of Night
She lost, alas! her wings of light;
When down, and down, and down she fell
'Mong scenes would rival Pollok's hell.

While falling, falling, naught could she
Save cloud on cloud of darkness see,
Yet on she sped her trackless way
Till Thought itself could not reach day.
She whizzing went adown so fast,
She feared 't would take her breath at last,
For still within Attraction's thralls,
The farther she, the faster falls.
At last she met loud, horrid moans
Which seem'd like Nature's dying groans.
She looks below and spies afar
Huge iron doors all set ajar,
And through them lurid flames of light
Burst forth upon her dizzy sight,
Whilst high above this burning world
Great clouds of smoke in anger curl'd;

From which arose such awful stench
As hell itself, she thought, would blench.
Destruction's jaws are opened wide
And waiting to receive their bride.
She plants herself in stern despair
To meet her doom—she's almost there—
Then gave one shriek when down she fell
Amid the burning fiends of hell.

The fiery billows o'er her roll;
With terror quakes her awe-struck soul.
O'er the red waves ride ghastly forms
Like floating drift when ocean storms.
She strained her eyes and with them tried
To see of hell the farthest side;
But vision's utmost reach attained
Ere half the distance it had gained,
Blind fell midway upon a throne
High, built of solid human bone,
Which well became who sat thereon.—
E'en the red roof above, so high,
She scarce could reach with vision's eye.
Great seas of fire roar and surge
Like Winter singing Autumn's dirge.
And brimstone mountains roof-high rise
Like melted gold before her eyes.
Strange, loathsome forms were panting seen
Of various size, and shape, and mien;
As various too, seem'd their employ:—
Some shrieked with pain, some laughed
    for joy;

Bot oh, such laugh! and oh, such shriek!
Would pale with fear e'en bravery's cheek.

Here serpents writhe, and twist, and turn,
And twist, and writhe, and hiss, and burn,
Enfolding each within its roll
The wasted form of some poor soul,
Like mighty Boa of the South,
When crushing prey to fill its mouth.
There horrid fiends, a countless throng,
Came dancing up through hell along,
All keeping time to music rung,
By wizard's hand and witch's tongue,
Till waves his wand the sooty king,
When ceased the clang, nor stirred one
        thing,
Except the fiery billows roll—
A solemn silence pained her soul.
"Ho, minions! Silence!"—list they all,
And prostrate on their faces fall—
"Ho, minions!" shouts a voice aloud
Like bursting of a thunder cloud—
"Release these new souls from the shroud,
In Tophet parlance give them greet,
And bind their hands, and bind their feet,
And by their tongues let them suspend
From yon high roof, time without end."

To do the bidding of their king,
Upon their feet they instant spring,

And send up such infernal yell
As shakes the very walls of hell.
The high behest anon obeyed;
The witches sung, the wizards played,
And on again, with whirl and prance,
Went merrily the fiendish dance.
But soon again the high command,
And wave of the Satanic wand,
In silence dread the scene enthral,
When loud again, resounds the call:
"Ho! heap more brimstone on the fire,
And let the flames of hell burn higher;
With human blood fill high the bowls.
Made from the skulls of human souls,
And drink a health to Hell's great king,
And louder let his praises ring."

Like thunder peals the yells resound;
The flowing bowls pass three times round.
With double zest they skip and prance,
And cross, and whirl, draw back, advance,
As onward speeds the giddy dance.

At length they spy her all unbound—
"Another soul!" the cry goes round,
When on they rush with yell and din,
Like nought beyond this den of sin.
They reach to grasp her trembling frame,
While higher booms the bursting flame.
She gave one shriek, and then awoke;
The dream was o'er, the spell was broke.

Bewildered, Alice ope'd her eyes,
And gazed her round in wild surprise.
Amazement perched upon her head,
Like boding fear when Hope is dead.
Belshazzar, feasting in his hall,
Read "*Mene tekel*" on the wall.
As plain she thought her doom she read,
And, like him, shook her frame with dread.
"Pray, what can such a vision mean?
Avaunt! thou gloomy, horrid scene!"
Quoth she: "My brother is not dead,
No murder rests on Willie's head.
My fears are traitors, and destroy
My hope, my peace, my ev'ry joy;
Pretending all the while to be,
Good friends advising how to flee
From some great curse o'erhanging me.
Then soul be calm, serene my breast,
Come balmy sleep, and give me rest."

PART II.

Again she sank in sweet repose,
When scenes of glory round her rose.
She thought she was an angel fair
With rainbow wings, and form of air.
Her flowing robes of snowy white,
Were fashioned from the sunbeams bright.

Her crown was crown of burnished gold,
On which her name was fair enrolled.
The moon-beam was her silver shoe,
The silken sky her mantle blue.
Her face was brighter than the sun's,
When not a cloud beneath him runs;
Yet milder, lovelier far to see,
Than Luna rising o'er the lea.

A world of glory and of light
Spreads out before her ravished sight.
She flaps her wings and parts the skies,
And off for it she instant hies:
Like sound, or sight, or thought she flies.
She nears it now and looks below,
The gates, with richest sapphire, glow.
The fields are white as morning snow,
When Phœbus rises from the sea,
Fresh bathed, and bright as bright can be.
While hills' and mounts' richest green,
Do variegate the dazzling scene.
Rich "floods of blossoms gliding on,"
Now instant seen, now instant gone,
All paint their image on her eye:
And streams of crystal wander by,
Bright as mirors made of steel
And pure as soul of saintly seal.
And groves unnumbered far around
Like seas of flow'rets flood the ground.

She looked above where met her eye
Great flocks of angels in the sky,

Like clouds of amber flitting by,
All wearing crowns of purer gold
Than eyes of mortals can behold;
And bearing palms of victory won
While dwelling far beneath the sun.
And hymning songs of endless praise
Which none but angel tongues can raise;
And fing'ring strings on harps of gold
Which none but angel hands can hold.
Her soul, ecstatic with such lays,
Arose and joined them in their praise;
Arose and joined the countless throng
And sped with them, like light, along.

They led her, quick as thought in dream,
To where there flowed a crystal stream—
The stream of Life which wanders by
The throne of Glory, white and high;
And dipt her body quickly in
To free her from the curse of sin.
They raised her from the rolling flood,
A thing immortal, pure, and good,
And fed her on ambrosial food.
They stript her of her robes of light,
And gave her robes of purer white.
A richer crown bedecked her head.
With finer wings she faster sped.
In her right hand a palm she bore;
Upon her breast a harp she wore;
She touched her finger to her tongue;
With angel voice she instant sung,

4

When all the host, a countless throng,
Sung hallelujahs loud and long;
And struck their harps, and waved their
      palms.
And sprinkled her with sweetest balms.
And silver-tongued seraphic cries
Of "Live forever! struck the skies."

They called her by a heavenly name,
Which mortal tongue can not proclaim :
And introduced her, young and coy,
To Hope, and Peace, and Love, and Joy
And all the countless hosts sublime,
That once had lived on shores of time :
And bade her dry, for aye the tear,
And bade her quake no more with fear;
Said, "black-winged woe, and keen-edged pain
Should ne'er molest her soul again."
Said, "sinners vile should meet their doom.
But she should smile in endless bloom."

They rose and led her far away,
To lands of everlasting day;
And yet no sun dispelled the night,
But endless floods of glory bright
Poured forth their radiant whirls of light.
She looked these lands of glory through;
Look where she would, the scene was new.
Here spread the rich ambrosial plains,
Where angel food, like manna, rains.
There rise the golden hills of God,
Where angels' feet ne'er yet have trod.

Proud Satan, once upon a time,
Essayed to scale these mounts sublime;
But, for presumptuous deed so fell,
They cast him into endless hell.

She saw a golden city there
Outshine the sun, so very fair
Its walls; and streets of precious stone
She saw; and saw Jehovah's throne,
From which burst forth, in glory bright,
Immortal founts of life, and light,
And trees of endless bloom were there,
All robed in beauty passing fair,
And bearing fruits of golden dyes,
Outsparkling brightest diamonds' eyes;
And spreading such perfume around,
As melts the soul in love profound.
Ten thousand rainbows deck the skies,
Where sun and clouds do never rise,
But there the sapphire dome of blue
Refracts the rays of glory true,
And spreads a mirror bright above,
Reflecting God in all His love.
But when she traced His image there,
So photographed, in glory fair
She shouted angel songs outright
And praised her Maker with her might.
So well she loved the high employ
Her soul was overcome with joy,
Which so disturbed her sleeping frame
From Fancy's land she hurrying came

And waked, with one convulsive scream,
Distressed to find it all a dream.

But soon regret, which on her face,
Sat like a cloud in gloomy grace,
To smiles of bright-eyed joy gave place,
New hope, like some great fount of light,
Burst forth upon her mental sight—
"The darksome future yet," quoth she,
"As bright as day may prove to me;
'The blackest hour of night,' some say,
'Comes just before the morning gray,'
And angriest clouds do often lie
Short space before the clearest sky."

THE SENTENCE.

Our long digression being o'er
We turn us to our tale once more.
Like Mississippi's turbid tide
Time's rushing stream doth swiftly glide,
And riding high that stream upon,
Stern Justice' court has come and gone.
And in its legal dignity
Has poised its equal scales on high
And deem'd that Willie Green must die.
The unrelenting sentence said
That he should hang till "*dead, dead, dead.*"
The charge on which he was arraigned
By evidence was well sustained.
The verdict of the jury read:
" *The price of blood is on his head.*"
His cheek was sunken now and pale
From long confinement in the jail,
But fear, remorse, nor guilt could chase
Bright innocence from his young face—
For no remorse or guilt was there
To stain his stainless character;
To tame his eye, his frame control,
Or stamp its impress on his soul.
Of firm and heaven-erected frame
He stood like monument of fame,
To vindicate his injured name.

His reason filed by danger's rasp,
With giant hold each point did grasp.
With demonstration plain and strong
And flowing speech he labored long
For trial new.   But Justice said:
" Thy evil deeds be on thy head.
The evidence of guilt 's too plain
To hear thy tedious cause again;
Nought now remains but to prepare
Thy soul by deep, repentant prayer
To stand before a sterner bar."

Each breath seemed held, the court-room
    still,
As silence on a midnight hill.
With more than Demosthenic pow'r,
Our hero stormed strong reason's tower,
And held entranced each nobler sense,
With silver-tongued, chaste eloquence.
His very soul seemed in his words,
So much he stirred the heart's soft cords.
Stern Justice dropped his scales and wept,
Revenge his dagger sheathed, and slept;
And Mercy stretched her tender hand
To lengthen out life's running sand;
While silken-robed, sweet-hearted Love,
Plead there with plaintive voice of dove;
Yet all could not avert his doom,
Or save him from the opening tomb.—

Oh! why should Nature's plastic hand
Uprear, with her omnific wand,

Such mighty prodigy of skill;
Then suffer Fate, with despot will,
To crumble it to dust again
Ere it has reached perfection's plane?
This query waive, momentous; deep;
Let Nature her own secrets keep,
For, "spite of pride," or "reason's spite,"
Pope says: "Whatever is, is right."

EMMA GLORE.

Short space from Willie turn again.—
In the poetic ville of N——,
Well known by some as "Silver Glen,"
There lived a beauteous, dark-haired maid,
Who came to give poor Alice aid;
To give the healing balm of peace,
And bid her dark, forboding cease;
To bid her sorrows calmly sleep
In fathomless Oblivion's deep.
Did this young maid perform her task?
We deem it now unmeet to ask.
But Alice said: "My heavy cares
Grew lighter daily, unawares."
Nor will we now of her say more
Than this: Her name was Emma Glore.

That she was young and passing fair,
With eyes of jet and raven hair;
Of form as good, and mien sublime,
As e'er were seen on shores of Time;
With soul as pure and head as sound
As love-sick swain e'er yet hath found;
With heart as warm and nature true,
As spotless virgin ever knew;
Yet, poor in wealth, she sought to aid
Young Alice as her waiting maid;
And more of her it yet may be
The sequel tells, as told to me.

THE EXECUTION.

Day rose in golden splendor bright,
And doffed the earth's black robes of Night.
And clothed her in rich floods of light.
Each brushy field, each glade and glen,
Each busy haunt of beast and men;
Each mountain top, each tow'ring spire
Is glittering now with living fire;
Whilst warbling songsters sing as sweet,
As if they nought but flow'rets eat,
All welcoming the god of day,
With unpremeditated lay—
The rattling wheels on streets of C——,
Rouse Willie from his reverie.
Amain he sprang upon his feet
And gazed adown the crowded street
Saying: "Happy C——, O! happy men,
I ne'er shall tread thy streets again!"

He paces now his narrow cell
As if enchanted by some spell;
Now mutters incoherent sounds;
The echoing wall the same rosounds;
Now turns and peeps 'twixt bar and bar
And sees uprearing high and far
His scaffold, from his prison room,
And seeing, reads his certain doom.

"Alas! alas! alas!" quoth he,
"How cruel, Fate, thou art to me!

Hadst thou but kept this woe at bay
Fair Alice' hand were mine to-day,
But now instead, of Death I 'm groom;
My wedding chamber is the tomb.
Yet Nature wears a smiling face
As if to mock at my disgrace.
'Mock those that can,' smile those that may,
This is my *execution day!*"

Already flocks the crowd around
The barb'rous execution ground,
And stretches far as vision's reach
Like rolling ocean on the beach.
This moving, mingling human tide
O'erflows each mound and hillock's side;
Each bough and bush in glade and glen
Is changing into forms of men.
The custom now become so rife
Each tree seems bearing fruit of life.—
Upon each limb and larger spray,
Like vultures waiting for their prey,
They hov'ring sit, and anxiously
Await the prisoner at the tree.

Time swiftly rolls the morning by;
Sol's chariot mounts the upper sky;
The town clock tolls the hour of ten,
The solemn sound each hill and glen,
On Echo's tongue returns again.
As dies the hour's sad knelling sound,
Far o'er the undulating ground,

One behind one, in solemn train,
Like lazy herd o'er western plain,
A slow procession winds along
To join the eager, motley throng.
Before it rolls a sable bier,
Bedewed by fond affections tear—
We need not lengthen out our verse
To tell who sat within the hearse.

"Make way! make way!" cries voice of storm,
"And let the prisoner reach the form!"
  This long procession from the lea
  Swells, as large rivers swell the sea,
  The crowd, and puts it in commotion,
  As swollen rivers do the ocean;
  But as the bird that parts the air
  Leaves on the sky no sign of scar;
  Or as the boat with plowing keel
  No furrow leaves behind its heel,
  So neither did the crowd retain
  One sign of opening by the train;
  But closed upon it as the wave
  Of ocean closes o'er the grave
  Of sinking ship.—The prisoner now
  Ascends the form, and with a bow
  The rabble greets. His garb was plain,
  For of his dress he ne'er was vain—
  Although his cheek was blanched and pale
  From long confinement in the jail,
  His model form and noble mien
  Still point him out as Willie Green.

He seem'd to say by his firm tread,
By his strong voice and stately head
"The sting of Death I do not dread."
His manner, looks, and self-control
Marked well his nobleness of soul;
For, one of Nature's nobles, he
From abject littleness was free.

His life blood flowed through better veins,
Through better heart and wiser brains,
Than oft is owned by men of state,
Whom chance or fortune has made great.
But to return—with graceful bow
We say, he greets the rabble now;
And in his *sui generis* style
He entertains it for awhile
With chaste, poetic, solemn speech
Which such as none but he can preach.
As twilight lulls the mind to sleep,
And lets the night in silence creep
Upon the slumb'ring earth; so now
Attention sits on ev'ry brow;
So now does silence most profound
Pervade this dark and bloody ground.
No sound is heard save what is flung
With force, from off his flow'ry tongue,
Or save, perchance, some mourning breeze,
Which softly weeps among the trees.—

The voice of eloquence can charm
The strong; the soldier brave disarm;

Can quake the coward's frame with fear;
From tender Marys draw the tear;
Can rouse the mob, or still its rage;
And calm hot youth, or fire old age.—

Two holy men, from neighboring town,
In white cravat and sable gown,
With love of God at heart, were there
Advice to give, and pray the prayer
Our Saviour prayed: "O! God forgive,
And let repentant sinners live.
Forgive our debts, O! God! as we
Forgive the prisoner at this tree."—

'T was Autumn, and the smoky sky
Half hid the sun's red, weeping eye.
Yes, Autumn—twilight of the year—
In sorrow bowed o'er Willie's bier,
And Nature doffs her robes of green,
In russet mourning to be seen.
"Her flinty cliffs and caverns lone
For her illustrious son make moan;
Her mountains weep in crystal rill,
Her flowers in tears of balm distill.
Through her brown groves the breezes sigh,
Her oaks in deeper groan reply;
And rivers teach their rushing wave
To weep around his gaping grave:
The field, the stream, the wood, the gale,
Is vocal with the plaintive wail."
And streams, like rivers, course the cheek,
Of hardy youth and maiden meek;

While matron old, and gray-haired sire
Feel, too, the scalding tear of fire.—

Again the startling town clock's toll
Admonishes the victim's soul
That, like the hour, he, too, will be,
Ere long, in dread eternity.—

But hark! A cannon's roar, aloud
Like thunder, bursts upon the crowd;
They noise-ward look, the curling smoke
At distance on their vision broke,
And on a townward hill they spy
A horseman waving flag on high;
All gazed upon the flying scene,
Much wondering what the flag could mean.
That it was commute or reprieve
Not one, a moment, could believe.
On comes the rider, on the steed,
Like rushing wind o'er rattling reed,
Nor hill, nor rock, nor ditch they heed
So fast they meet and part the wind,
So quickly leave each scene behind,
That flag and cloak play on the breeze,
Like streamers on the open seas.
The noble steed flew on so fast,
Rock, glen, and hill like magic passed;
While, from his well-tried, clatt'ring shoe,
Bright sparks of fire like lightning flew.

"Hold, hangman, hold!" a voice from far
Bursts on each ear like voice of war.

While harder plies the rider's heel,
And deeper strikes the gory steel.

"Hold, hangman, hold!" the voice again
Comes echoing o'er the uneven plain.
Speed, rider, speed! three minutes more,
(Forbid it heaven), and all is o'er.
On flies the steed with open mouth,
And panting breath, while soapy froth
In feath'ry drops rolls off below,
Like frosty flakes of falling snow.
The crowd excited much to see
The rider dash so fearlessly
O'er ragged rock and rolling rill;
O'er grassy dale and bushy hill,
On curious tiptoe stand agape,
And closely eye the coming shape.
At last, the rushing twain draw nigh;
The rider stands in stirrup high,
And shouts in stentor peals aloud:
"Make way! make way! make way! the
        crowd!
Hold, hangman hold! Much rather I,
Than my best friend on earth should die!"
The horseman slackens now the reins;
Slow pacing up the crowd he gains,
And waves the flag but three times round
When horse and rider strike the ground.
The faithful beast all covered o'er
With mud, and foam, and clotted gore,
Now gasping lies to rise no more.

And fainting too the rider lies
All motionless with half-closed eyes,
And thready pulse, and lab'ring breath:
O! stay thy hand, relentless Death!

The sheriff took the flag in charge,
And on it read, in letters large,
In voice that echoed o'er the down.
The welcome name of *"Allen Brown!"*

Now tears of joy stole down glad eyes,
And shouts of rapture rent the skies.
The stranger rises from the ground
And wildly staring him around
Cries: "Hangman, listen thou to me
And set the cord-bound prisoner free.
I'm Allen Brown, from foreign tour
Returning to my native shore."

So much his make and mien had changed
Since o'e his native hills he'd ranged,
The Major swore 't was not his son
And bade the bloody work go on.
"Release his neck! By heaven I swear,
I am the Brown whom you declare,
Through hate, or pride, or fit of spleen,
Was paled in death by Willie Green!
Why stand ye longer in suspense
When I declare his innocence?"

The rabble now, a sea of fire,
Are stirred against young Allen's sire,

And vow that he shall feel the smart
Well aimed by him at nobler heart.
They seized the rope that Willie wore,
And, in their wrath, most hotly swore
That he, as Haman did, when caught,
Should eat the fruit his labor bought.
But Willie rose above the storm
And loud harangued the furious swarm,
And soon the raging sea was still
As twilight on a western hill.
Meet consultation being held
The prisoner was forthwith re-celled
In C——'s secure and gloomy jail
To hear in court the stranger's tale.

THE WITCH.

Now Lady Green was made to feel
The weight of persecution's heel,
For it was held, by some, that she
Well knew the art of sorcery;
That by the aid of Satan's pow'r
She could evoke, in danger's hour,
The foulest fiend that roasts in hell,
And make him seem on earth to dwell;
Aye, make him seem a king or clown,
Or take the form of Willie Brown.
Some deemed, indeed, her hellish plot
As great as those of Michael Scott;
That she could spell their peaceful glens
As he did Oakward's dales and dens;
And that some freak which she had played
Raised Allen Brown from Hadean shade,
As Samuel was by Endor's aid.
So high rose passion's tide, at length
That in their blindness, zeal, and strength
They dragged her up the clan before,
As sapients did in days of yore,
And poised the scales of Justice well
To see if she were leagued with hell.
Her person in one scale was placed,
A bible large the other graced.

Each proem fixed with honest care
The holy book rose high in air,
In tongueless language to declare
Her innocence, and set her free
From ignorant credulity.
They quickly gave her a release
And bade her go her way in peace. †

The stranger's proof—to some severe—
Was, as a sunbeam, strong and clear.
Each circumstance of strong array
Like morning frost-work passed away.
The rays of truth shone on each mind
Till prejudice, though almost blind,
Could see through his beclouded veil
The fallacy of error's tale.
Till doubt, with tongue unwav'ring, said:
"The lost is found; yet lives the dead;"
Till city gent and country clown
Admit the stranger's Allen Brown,
When fly the prison doors ajar
And Willie Green's as free as air.

---

† This test for witchcraft was used by a Scotch magistrate, against a woman, thirty miles back of Cincinnati, Ohio, as late as the year 1809.

THE FAREWELL

Like restless deer, from man set free,
He trips it o'er the streets of C——,
And with a heart more grave than gay.
He homeward wends his anxious way,
Revolving whether he should see
His Alice fair, or from her flee.
Quoth he, at length: "Like Cain I'll hie
To some far Nod, in peace to die.
How can I, covered with disgrace,
Show Alice Brown my shameful face?
How can I, fresh from gallows stand,
Essay to claim her heart and hand?
How can I, with my bosom torn,
My mind depressed, and hope forlorn,
Remain where all my sorrows grew?
From whence my joys all winged flew.

"Land of my youth, farewell! farewell!
Thou hast become a burning hell!
Farewell, Ohio! deep and wide,
Whose soft blue waters gently glide—
Regardless of Earth's care and strife—
Like the last days of well-spent life.
Could I but sing thee just and true;
Thy hills, and dales, and mountains blue;

Thy graceful windings, thy sweet roar;
As on thy waters calmly pour,
Thy meadows green and forests wild,
Thou Nature's truest, loveliest child,
No greater boon I'd ask, save one,
While thy sweet waters onward run—
But this I may not even name;
The thought consumes me like a flame.—
O! mount my soul! where thy desire
Can boldly grasp an angel's lyre!
Or this refused, give me to ask
Some gifted muse to aid my task;
Yet granted this, e'en then my heart
Would fail to sing thee as thou art.

"Could Byron, Scott, or Robert Burns
But rise them from their mouldering urns,
They'd sing thee greater than the Clyde
With scenery grand, and even tide;
Than Yarrow, Dundee, or the Tyne,
Already sung in strains so fine.
Not 'Tweed's fair river, broad and deep.'
Could bear thy laurels from the cheap.
O! classic stream! adieu! adieu!
To thee and all thy glory true!
Farewell, my cot! my humble home!
I tear me from thee now to roam,
Far from thy wide inviting door
Mayhap to greet thy walls no more!
Thy fading groves, my aching heart,
Tell me how loth we are to part.

'Farewell, my friends! farewell, my foes!
My peace with these; my love with those!'"
Thus saying, hard he homeward pressed;
His mother's form son-like caressed;
Placed her above the tyrant, Want,
Which, like a vampire, lean and gaunt,
Sat ready to insert his beak
And draw the life-blood from her cheek.
He bade her be of happy cheer,
And for his welfare have no fear,
Then brushed the tear-drop from his eye,
And looked a sad, though fond, "good-bye."
But, of this matter now no more;
The painful parting pass we o'er,
And leave the absent one to tell
Things other which the while befell.—

Soon long-tongued Rumor spread the tale,
That Willie eastward had set sail,
With full intent life's bark to moor
On far Australia's golden shore.
But when fair Alice came to hear,
The flight of him she deemed so dear,
Her soul again was drowned in fear.

Fresh cups of sorrow deep she drains,
And feels its poison chill her veins,
Her constant heart more closely clung
To him whom wrong so deeply stung,
And hunted down with sland'rous tongue.

Her feeble frame, which ill could brook
The dangers of so great a shock,
Seemed tottering, now, with failing breath,
O'er the stupendous steep of death.
Like some desponding, mateless dove,
She sorrowed thus her absent love;—

A SOLILOQUY.

"I little thought that I should be
The cause of so much misery;
That, for my sake, my father's heart
From honor's laws should e'er depart.
And bring the idol of my soul
So near an ignominious goal.
That idol, too, I little thought,
To sense of shame, could e'er be brought.
I know he hath a conscience clear,
Why, then, weak maiden, doth he fear?
How could he thus his country flee,
And leave his home to woe and me?
Could he suppose that I will prove
Disloyal to my only love?

"When Satan, from his nether throne,
Came up and marked thee for his own,
Did not my heart then bleed for thee?
And, bleeding, show its constancy?
The changing moon may wane and grow;
Inconstantly the tides may flow:
Attraction may its force resign,
May cease the dazzling sun to shine,
But ne'er shall change this heart of mine.
"What happy days and joys I knew,
Ere troubles' arrows pierced me through!

Destroyed were these, restored were those,
On lightning wings would flee my woes.
Then were this earth a heaven to me,
Then sorrows would but pleasures be;
Those happy joys! those happy days!
Fond mem'ry still around them plays!

"O! happy joys, forever dead!
O! happy days, forever fled!
Where are your faces now! O, where!
My bursting heart can you declare?
Gone, like a melting April snow,
That falls where gliding waters flow!
Gone, like the setting sun's last beam,
And left me of the past to dream!
Aye, gone with all my hopes, alas!
Like sweet, young blades of tender grass
Before chill Autumn's blighting frost!
Yes, gone for aye! forever lost!

"O! could I Willie's footsteps trace,
On wings of love I'd seek his face!
Nor e'er give o'er the pleasing task
Till, as of yore, my heart could bask
In the sweet sunshine of his smiles,
And free itself from woe's turmoils!" —

TRUST IN GOD.

"Thy useless wailings pray give o'er,"
  Said the sweet voice of Emma Glore.
"The future yet may have in store
  Rich wells of bounless joy for thee,
  Fair Alice, as thou yet mayst see.

"There is a God who dwells on high;
  Omnipotent; who can not lie;
  Who rules the earth, and sea, and sky:
  The drop, the gnat, the smallest mite,
  The greatest good: therefore rules right.
  Unnumber'd worlds, through boundless space,
  As He designs, their orbits trace.
  Nor did the greatest ever prove
  An overmatch for Him above.
  Then how can things on earth transpire
  Contrary to His vast desire?

"If God, omnipotent, shapes our ends,
  Rough hew them as we may; and sends
  What, unto us, as evil seems,
  And sending this most fitly deems
  It for our good, it must be so,
  For goodness, only, can he do.
"Since He hath ordered thee to drain
  The cup of sorrow and of pain,

It must be right—why, then, repine?
Or murmur at His will divine?
How could sweet roses ever bloom
And scent the air with their perfume;
Or charm us with their ruddy blush,
If 't were not for the thorny bush?
And 't were not for our pain and woe,
How could we aught of pleasure know?
Then train your faith as train you should;
' All evil terminates in good.'

"Then cheer thee, cheer thee, weeping maid,
And hie thee from doubt's blighting shade.
A sun of hope e'en now doth shine
Through disappointment's foggy shrine;
And if thou wilt but ope thine eyes,
Thou yet mayst see the fairest skies.
Compare thy lot dear maid, with mine,
No longer canst thou then repine.
Here, golden wealth comes at thy beck,
With beads of diamond round his neck.
His person robed in rich array,
To do thy bidding day by day.
And mother kind and father strong,
Stand by to bay the monster wrong.
Whilst all thy friends, a num'rous host,
Seem trying who shall aid thee most.

But I, of wealth, or friends have none,
Or kindred left beneath the sun,
No, ne'er did wealth, his couch of ease,
Spread out, obsequious, me to please,

And ere learned I to lisp the name
Of parents, on pale horse there came
An angel black, whose name is Death,
And laid them both the sod beneath.
And O! my kindred where are they?
Go, ask the worms that on them prey!
My friends are fled like morning dew,
And left the orphan here with you.
Yet calm in soul, serene in mind,
I am unto my fate resigned."—

"It is enough," the mourner said,
"For very shame I hang my head.
Yet if the fates me only spare,
Before high heaven do I declare,
That I will seek my Willie's face
If I can e'er his footsteps trace."—

The low'ring cloud of wrath gone by;
Once more restored a peaceful sky;
The sentence void; the prisoner free,
Soon homeward hastens Allen B——
Impatient for his loved abode,
He winds the old familiar road.
Joy throbbed his pulse, high rose his breast,
As nearer to his home he pressed.
Each hill and glade, each rill and stone,
Reminds him of old pleasures gone.

THE SURPRISE.

The sacred place at length he nears;
Joy bathes his manly eyes in tears.
Old groves he meets, and dulcet streams;
Old mem'ries crowd his brain with dreams;
The house he spies, the fields, the lane,
And lives his boyhood o'er again.

Almost four years of time have flown,
Since last he stood that spot upon;
"Old times were changed," and so was he,
Since he a tourist came to be.
The awkward form of other days
Was now well schooled to courtly ways.
Improved in manner and in word,
With bearing like some noble lord,
He deemed it no great task to clown
Himself as strange to Alice Brown.

A maiden in the grove he spies,
And thought his sister to surprise,
By fig'ring in his foreign guise.
Dismissed his horse, dismissed his man,
Up through the grove he slyly ran,
And taking stand behind a tree,
Long stood agape this maid to see.
So great his wonder and surprise,
He scarce believed his ravished eyes.

Those jetty curls so like the crow,
Which played in such delightful flow
Around her neck and breast of snow,
No whit of true resemblance bore
To the rich auburn Alice wore.

He knew his sister's eyes of blue,
Could never take so dark a hue;
And when the song "Sweet Home" she sung,
The silver cadence from her tongue,
All through the grove like magic rung.
He thought of harps in fairy land
And almost viewed one in her hand.
The more he gazed, the more admired,
Till his young breast with love was fired.
His heaving heart enraptured beat;
His soul lay prostrate at her feet.

So great the workings of his breast,
A sigh half heaved and half suppressed,
Fell lightly on her list'ning ear,
When to her feet, like timid deer,
Much wrought upon by sudden fear,
She instant sprang and lovely stood,
The graceful nymph of *Eden Wood*,
In all her beauty full-revealed,
Which until then was half-concealed.
As from the tree the stranger tread,
A meet excuse he fitly made,
And softly to the maiden said:
"I hasten from a foreign strand
Once more, to see my native land."

Her startled face and dancing eye,
Showed her first impulse was to fly;
But, glancing at the stranger's form,
Upon his face she read "no harm,"
For, forms like his, when maiden's see,
They seldom wish, if e'er to flee.
With bounding heart, and head aside,
To rein her tongue, for speech she tried,
That love's strange passion she might hide;
Which passion she the more concealed,
Itself the plainer but revealed.
'T was thus her feelings inly strove,
As proud she stood amid the grove,
A blushing monument of love.

At length the painful silence broke,
She thus unto the stranger spoke:
"A stranger from a foreign shore,
Returning to thy home once more,
The same, no doubt, we mourn as dead."
"The very same," the stranger said;
"Then haste the back to C——'s fair town,
And seek thy sister, Alice Brown,
Who fled this day to parts unknown.—"

Cast down with grief, the stranger said:
"Ill luck on my devoted head."
Then mansion-ward they slowly turned,
When soon his partner's name he learned—
"A sister I have lost," thought he:
"May I another find in thee;

I 've stood on Europe's distant shore,
And cast my eyes her beauty o'er;
Not there did such fine flow'ret bloom
As find I at my native home.
Ten thousand maidens have I seen,
From rustic lass to stately queen,
Yet ne'er beheld mine eyes before
Such lovely form as Emma Glore."—
But when he learned her lowly grade,
Passed o'er his brow a gloomy shade;
He loved his sister's waiting maid.—

"O, Love! thou king of soul and sense!
Against whose shaft is no defense!
Thou tender tyrant of mankind!
Thou ruler of the heart and mind!
How great thy silken sceptred sway
O'er us poor mortals of a day!"—
Thought Allen, as his father's door
Oped, welcome to his beck once more.—

" The peasant feels thy silken cords;
Thy power o'ercomes earth's noblest lords;
While kings bow down before thy shrine,
And angels own thy sway divine.
Since all their heads before thee lower,
Can I escape thy wondrous power?
Can I annul thy warm decrees,
And guide thy passion as I please?
If not, why feed ambition's pride?
Why spurn this orphan from my side?

She fills 't is true, a lowly sphere,
But Nature makes her my compeer.
How oft the wealthy, pompous, great,
Who boast of titles, power, and state,
But will not thee, O! Love! confess,
Are wanting in true happiness!

" What 's pomp or honor at the best?
Oft Mis'ry in rich color 's drest.
Behold the boy with dextrous skill,
Breathe lightly through his soapy quill;
Behold his peacock bubbles rise,
Expanding in the airy skies!
But ere his fortune's fully blown,
It bursts, and all its glory 's gone:
The mourning hero left alone.

So honor, with its dreams of gold,
Bursts ere its pleasures half unfold,
And leaves us but the quill to hold.
Then, since my lot has been to see,
For honor's sake such misery
I'll shun the rock where thousands wreck,
And learn ambition wild to check.
I bow, O! Love! thy shrine before;
I will not spurn thee, Emma Glore."

His thoughts no further now pursue,
But leave him in home's bosom true,
To drink from wells of blissful joy
Parental sweets without alloy.

6

Short halt at home, howe'er, he made,
But hied anon to lend his aid
In searching o'er the diff'rent routes
His absent sister's whereabouts.
Wide was the search, and long as wide,
But whate'er Alice did betide,
Prediction's tongue could ill surmise,
Nor prescience see with all his eyes.

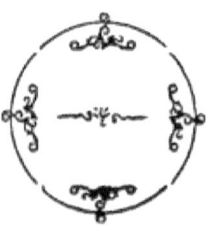

THE LOVED AND LOST.

Chilled by remorse and mis'ry's frost,
The parents mourned their child as lost,
When russet Autumn's glories fled;
"When grief grew calm and hope was dead;"
When expectation's heart beat low;
When sorrow's tears had ceased to flow,
Was found beneath a sheet of snow,
Far in a wide and lonely glade,
The fragile form of some poor maid.

Stern Winter, from his icy throne,
Had touched and turned her frame to stone,
And wound her in her shroud of white,
To spend a long and gloomy night,
Without a tear to wet her tomb;
She slept unknowing and unknown:
Her death knell was the cavern's groan:
Her dirge the howling wind's shrill moan.

Some sportsmen, in pursuit of game,
By chance, across the sleeper came,
They saw her auburn ringlets spread
In wild confusion round her head,
And found her slender female form
Snow-buried by the winter storm.
Two solemn blasts from their loud horn,
The scattered hunters thither warn.

Expecting sport, fast, man by man,
Came rushing in the summoned clan.
But who can tell, or who surmise.
Their sudden feeling of surpise,
On seeing stretched, when up they came,
A stiffened corpse, instead of game.

When from its icy coffin raised
The silent huntsmen, much amazed.
In silent recognition gazed,
Upon this proof of former life.
In Death's embrace—his wedded wife—
Till one, at last, the silence broke,
And words of interchange were spoke.
When ev'ry voice within the down,
Cried out, as one' "'T is *Alice Brown!*"—

How fast the eagle parts the air;
How nimbly flees the timid deer;
How quick the eye strikes ether's blue;
How fast new thoughts the old pursue.
As fast as new thoughts old ones trace;
As fast as vision measures space;
More swiftly than the roebuck hies,
And faster than the eagle flies
Bad news, on lightning wings, doth wind
From mouth to mouth, from mind to mind;
For scarcely had one short day died
Since the mysterious dead was spied,
Ere all the nearest neighb'ring land
Together met, in solemn band,

And placed her in a stately tomb
Prepared at her own father's home,
To sleep till judgment bids her bloom.
So heavy was the grievous stroke,
Her mother's tender heart soon broke;
Now child and mother, side by side,
In Death's pale city both abide.

The father bowed his humbled head,
And thus unto himself he said:
" Here lies the wreck my rashness wrought!
Ah! dear 's the school where I was taught!
Ah, woe is me! my daughter 's dead!
And, with her, my last joy has fled!
May I forget the cursed day
When cursed rashness made me say
'That Alice Brown shall ne'er be seen
The spouse of such as Willie Green!'
Too true my vow hath come at last!
Oh, God, forgive me for the past!
Could I but now reverse her doom,
And paint her cheek with Hygia's bloom,
Ere she should flee—despite my spleen—
I 'd give her hand to Willie Green."—

The woodman's ax may wound the tree,
But yet the gash will healed be,
And scarce a scar remain to see.
The deepest pangs the heart can feel,
Time's suaging ointment oft will heal;
But what can heal thy wounds, remorse?
Or what avert their crushing force?

What conscience can endure the sting
Thy poisoned arrows with them bring?

The curtain drops o'er this sad scene,
But let us hear from Willie Green;
Who, as we have already said,   .
Was so berought with shame and dread,
That from fair Alice' face he fled.
His heaving soul with anguish burned,
As from his home his footsteps turned.

THE WANDERER.

Now tempest-toss'd on life's rough tide,
Without a compass, or a guide,
He steered for some uncertain shore,
Expecting to return no more.
Town after town he northward meets;
Scene after scene his vision greets,
Yet rest for mind nor foot he finds,
As on his wand'ring course he winds;
Until at last the weary youth,
Betakes him to the sunny South,
Where, like the cypress, or the date,
He plants himself, and soon grows great.

Poetic was the spot he chose,
At which to stop and court repose.
'T was not where, with his mouth oped wide,
The Mississippi spits his tide,
And disembogues his mud and sand
Upon old Mexic's gulfy strand;
Or where his rushing, mighty wave
Rolls o'er De Soto's wat'ry grave;
Nor was it where the southron spies
The Crescent City steeples rise
To point him to his native skies.
'T was where a grove of walnut trees
Once spread its branches to the breeze,

And sweetened, with its lungs, the air
By breathing out its fragrance there;
Where hill on hill, in beauty piled,
And washed their feet in brooklets wild,
As purled they down each steep ravine,
Which dug itself those hills between.
'T was where a stately thriving town
In all its southern pride looks down,
From her high-rising throne supreme,
On Mississippi's rushing stream.
Yes, Vicksburg, on her hills like Rome,
He chose for his adopted home.

Nor had he long resided there,
Before his genius, rich and rare,
Burst forth, a glorious noon-day sun,
Unnumb'red spell-bound minds upon;
And all who felt its magic blaze
Confessed the power of its rays.

We said "his ever-active mind
To useful study was inclined,"
E'en prison walls could not destroy
His innate love for this employ.
'T was then, we said, "he journey'd o'er
The fertile fields of legal lore;"
'T was standing thus, 'twixt death and life,
He trained his mind for legal strife;
And when removed to southern town,
His mighty powers soon were known.

He proved himself, in ev'ry cause,
A perfect Blackstone in the laws.§

So wide his reputation spread,
That honor's crown soon wreathed his head.
So great his clients deemed his skill,
Began his coffers soon to fill ;
And scarce had three years trod Time's strand,
When wealth stretched forth his golden hand,
And waved o'er him his glittering wand,
And bade him call on him for aid,
To further schemes ambition laid.

But scarce gained he one giddy flight
On honor's mount, ere some new height
Before him rose, his soul to fire,
And make him for its top aspire.
His laurels gained, he cast behind,
And forward pressed, fresh fame to find.
Wen six and twenty years of age,
Affairs of state his mind engage ;
He mounts the politician's stage,
And with his great Websterian brain
He storms each heart, and stirs each vein.
The list'ning throngs with rapture fill,
And lavish praises on his skill.

Long was the fight for place, and hard,
But merit reaped, for him, reward ;

---

§This part of the tale is founded on the legal and political
career of S. S. Prentiss,

And gave a seat in Congress Hall
To him who most deserved the call;
But when arrived at Washington
A second battle was begun:
For some there were who deemed that he
Obtained his seat illegally.
With mental weapons polished bright,
He rushed again into the fight:
And plucked fresh laurels of renown,
From heads that wore bright honor's crown.
For three long days he faced the foe;
For three long days like rivers flow,
Bright gems of wisdom from his tongue,
The White House walls unchecked along;
While crowded round his form there stand
The pride and glory of the land.

Astonished at the youth unpeered,
And at the eloquence they heard,
So fired were all by Nature's child,
The Nation's mighty heart beat wild,
And danced true time to music rung
From off his Demosthenic tongue.

The Sage of Ashland rose to tell
How much his heart the youth did spell;
And Marshfield's son for very joy,
Encomia lavished on the boy;
*And Carolina's tallest pine
Fell down and worshipped at his shrine.

---

*Clay, Webster, and Calhoun.

The halls were vocal with his praise;
All cried "Success and length of days!"
His enemies began to beat
From battle-field, a quick retreat,
And let him take, in peace, his seat.

The session o'er, he hied anon
For far Australia to be gone,
In search of her from whom he fled,
And whom her father mourned as dead;
For he had learned at Washington
That thither fled his Alice Brown,
In hopes to see her Willie's face,
If she could e'er his footsteps trace.

From New York's crowded port he sails,
Before propitious, steady gales,
Upon a gently rolling sea,
Whose bosom heaving seemed with glee.
Their vessel, graceful as the swan,
Sat proudly the blue waves upon;
Spread her white wings, the breeze before,
And gaily flew the waters o'er.
"All went," so charming was the spell,
As "merry as a marriage bell,"
Until Pacific's maddened wave
Forewarned them of a watery grave.

The foaming billows, mountain high,
Seemed touching near the angry sky,
While, like a frightened thing of life,
The craft, too weak to stem the strife,

Was hotly chased o'er ocean's breast,
By raging storms far to the west.
With rigging rent, and compass lost,
For months on months they 're tempest tost,
Upon a boundless aqueous field,
To all aboard as unrevealed
As if they had, of late, been hurled
Into some new and unknown world.

At last the faithful ship " Relief"
Was driven on a coral reef,
Which, 'neath the wave concealed lay,
Like some gigantic fish of prey,
To swallow down the hapless sail,
Sent thither by mad Neptune's gale.
She wrecked upon this rocky strand,
In sight of some inviting land;
When all, beneath the surging wave,
Save Willie, found a wat'ry grave;
And he, so troubled was his breast,
" Wished to be with them, and at rest."
Yet, when the raging storm was o'er,
On floating fragments sought the shore,
And, on his bended knees, did there
Pour out his soul in thankful prayer. .

‖ Pelew's sweet isles, all clothed in green,
About him lay—a rapt'rous scene—
Upon the ocean's rocking breast,
Like sleeping babes just lulled to rest.

‖ See Captain Wilson's account of his shipwreck upon the Pelew Islands.

The orange and the lemon bloom,
Were there to charm with their perfume;
And warbling songsters plumed in gold,
In dulcet chains his senses hold;
And rolling mounts which prop the sky
Paint grandeur on his wond'ring eye,
And silver lakes and crystal streams,
Before him sport, like plessant dreams.
And ocean's constant bass keeps time
To Sylva's dulcet strains sublime.
Bright Phœbus, in his golden car,
Slow rolling down the west afar,
Seems sinking into ocean's breast,
As weary trav'ler seeking rest.
Above high domes soft ether's blue,
An upper ocean to the view.
While Neptune's waves beneath him ire,
One dazzling sheet of flashing fire,
Creating, as they burnished roll,
An emblem of his troubled soul.

"Oh! what a view is here," quoth he,
  As gazed he round him pensively.
"Oh! what a scene is here, my heart,
  For poet's pen or painter's art!
  Can all the works of human pride
  With thee compare?" he softly cried.
"Could Adam's lovely paradise
  More charm the true admirer's eyes?
  Here Nature scatters, free and wild,
  Her rugged hills and valleys mild.

"Arrayed are these, in flow'rets fair;
Embalming, with their breath, the air,
On those, in waving forests, stand,
As emblems of a fertile land,
The bread-tree and the cocoa tall;
The pride of lovely Artingall.*

"Here Nature's roughest pastures are;
Beauty and grandeur mingle there,
So wild, so strange, 'the whole doth seem,
The scenery of a fairy dream.'
But ah! yon crowing cock doth tell
Of childhood's joys, remembered well;
Of earlier, happier, sweeter hours,
Known ere I knew misfortune's powers.
My native land 's my own no more;
Destined am I, on this lone shore,
A woeful anchorite, to brood
O'er pleasures dead, in solitude.
I seem, without a foe, to stand
As Crusoe did, on Juan's land,
The ruling monarch of the strand.
Yet all this kingdom would I give
Could I but with my Alice live!
O! that my heart were flint or steel,
That mis'ry's pang I might not feel!

"But I bethink me now, 't is well
No longer on such themes to dwell.

---

* Artingall is one of the Pelew Islands.

The golden rays of ebbing day
Have ceased to light me on my way.
The pulse of Nature standeth still;
Now Night's dark mantle hides each hill.
Each beast doth claim itself a bed,
But I 've 'not where to lay my head.'
Yon floating gull e'en seeks her nest
And I must lay me here to rest.
This grassy isle my couch must be;
The sky's blue dome, my canopy."—

Thus saying, on the friendly ground,
In slumber's chains he soon was bound;
But ill could Morpheus lull to rest
The ruling passions of his breast.
In fitful dreams, before him rose,
Shipwrecks and perils, full of woes.
Now on some stormy ocean toss'd,
His vessel, crew, and friends are lost.
Next, on Columbia's distant strand,
Among his friends he seems to stand.
An aged mother there he sees
And falls before her on his knees.

Now smiles and cries: "O! God, I 'm blest!"
And clasps his Alice to his breast;
And now a gloomy prison door
Opes up his troubled mind before.
To Vicksburg, friendless, next he came,
An angler in the tide of fame;
And next, to please his party's call,
He proudly stands in Congress hall,

And bravely fights the battles o'er
He had so bravely fought before.
Again he passed o'er childhood's youth:
Sweet years of sunshine and of truth:
And words of friendship interchanged
With those ten thousand miles estranged.

Now pass his friends before his mind;
The loved, the faithful, and the kind.
At length his Alice with her charms,
He spies in some strange lover's arms.
His heart beat low, his hope was fled—
He raised him from his dewy bed,
And saw the morning's scarf of red,
And heard sweet birds on sprig and spray
With music hail the new-born day.
He rose, returning thanks to God,
And onward plods his unknown road.

On dreamy Pelew's distant isle,
Leave we young Willie for a while,
And far across the boiling main,
We homeward steer our bark again,
To learn, perchance, some small jot more,
Of Allen Brown and Emma Glore.

ALLEN AND EMMA.

Ambitious pride and blinded love,
In Allen's breast alternate strove;
This seemed, to-day, supreme to reign,
To-morrow that, new force, would gain.
Within his soul, so great the strife,
Grew dim, at length, his lamp of life:
For fled his joys; his peace was gone;
Strong reason tott'r'd on its throne.

But, as the constant beams of day,
Will melt the deepest snow away,
And swell the seeds to grass and grain,
Which, in the earth had frozen lain,
So did the smiles of Emma's face
Make wint'ry pride to love give place.
The heaving storm was lulled to rest,
That raged within his troubled breast.

Began his heart to melt and run
Beneath the rays of Hymen's sun.
Again his bosom felt the glow
Of Hygia's life-preserving flow.

Returned once more his peace and joy,
For Emma's care was his employ.
'T were long to tell the wooings o'er
'Twixt Allen Brown and Emma Glore.

7

Now, in the wild, inviting groves,
They oft pursued their happy loves;
How warm his suit, his hopes, how high;
How blushed her cheek, how danced her eye;
How like two sprigs of eglantine,
Their willing souls in one combine;
Aye, twine and mingle into one,
Beneath true-love's soft summer sun.

How maiden's eyes, of high degree,
Met his, in vain, for sympathy.
How she, all blushing as a rose,
Was wooed, in vain, by countless beaux;
And, how admired, the country through,
Her diamond eyes, rich set in dew:
But pass we this, for it were vain,
To lengthen this, our closing strain.

That true love's course, 't is said, in sooth,
Since time began ne'er did run smooth.
A mixture, but of storm and calm;
A thorn to-day, to-morrow balm;
But be this false, or be it true,
As soon as Major Brown well knew
His son's affections thus to be
Placed on this maid of mean degree,
His iron heart and Shylock soul
Could scarce be kept within control.
His leaden eye, of sullen scorn,
Looked angry as a winter morn.
In vain his friends around him press,
His better judgment to address,

He, like some love-forsaken swain,
Seemed racked in sense, and racked in brain.
'T were well had he, in hoary age,
Seasoned his acts with judgment sage,
For sixty winters, as they fled,
Their snows had scatt'red o'er his head;
Yet, like some peevish, fretful child
His burning passion drove him wild.
At length, howe'er, calmed down his rage,
Like wintry winds at twilight's stage,
And sober thoughts his mind engage;
And o'er the old man's face there play
Smiles approbative, bland as day.

But ah, that calm! and ah, those smiles!
Were but a devil's cunning wiles.
Such calms we often see, in form,
Between two bursts of thunder storm;
Such smiles the cat would give in play,
Ere the poor mouse it stoops to slay—

Quoth Brown, concealing, with true art,
The impulse real of his heart:
" 'T were well, my son, should you give o'er,
Awhile, your marriage with Miss Glore.
Should you one year with me abide,
I swear, by heaven, whate'er betide,
She then shall be your loving bride,
And all my wealth shall subject be
To foster one of your degree;
But slight you, sir, this offer now,
And penniless you from me go."

So pleased with hopes of compromise,
The son's confiding, honest eyes
Could not detect the latent fire
That smoulder'd still within the sire,
And threatened, with volcanic pow'r,
To burst, and all his hopes devour.

"It is enough," young Allen said,
And in submission bowed his head.
"Though long the time and hard the task,
Your son will do the thing you ask."

As noiseless as a spirit's tread,
On lightning wings time swiftly fled;
Nor fled too fast—expectant love
Still faster wished the hours to move.
Though busy was the tick of time;
Not busier than the sons of crime.
The father's breast, of conscience void,
Left no devices unemployed.
He was resolved, if such could be,
To make the lover's disagree.

First, by persuasion, soft and strong,
He tried full hard, and tried full long,
To master him, he fain would rule
By iron rod of servile school.
Mild measures proved of no avail,
On each was plainly written "*fail.*"
Then slander next, "foul whelp of sin,"
Stuck her long tongue the business in;
And with full might and main long strove,
To nip the bud of tender love.

Reports crept out, and passed for true,
"That virtue Emma Glore ne'er knew;
That virtue's name she scarce could boast,
So long her honor had been lost."

Each wily hint was guarded well,
With "how," or "when," or "who can tell?"
Yet it was plain, as many said,
That shame sat brooding o'er her head.—

Snail-like doth Virtue plod her mile,
But Vice, rough shod, runs twain the while,
So those who scarce had heard the name
Of this poor maid, now puffed her shame;
But Allen could not yet believe
That she would "practice to deceive."
As well might quail on eagle prey;
Or try the lamb the wolf to slay,
As for the sire to make the son
Believe the tale vile slander spun.—

Such confidence can love bestow,
We scarce can lay the passion low—
But howsoe'er it was agreed
That demonstration should proceed,
To make the matter clear and plain,
And render future doubting vain.
'Twas told that Emma did receive
A paramour each Sabbath eve,
Who took her to his lech'rous arms,
And reveled in her maiden charms,

Till dappled dawn made haste to warn
The soft approach of gray-eyed morn.—

One ev'ning down the garden strolled—
As blushing twilight ebbing rolled
A silver sea of fading day—
Young Allen in his habit gay.
Dull silence wide her mantle spread,
O'er hill, and dale, and mountain's head;
And Nature's soul seemed calmed to rest
On the still waves of Night's dark breast.
The folding rose, in modest bloom,
Sweet welcome gave with its perfume.
The coriander's pleasant balm,
A greeting sent, beneath the calm.
The laughing, sparkling, starry crew,
Peeped forth from out their windows blue,
All radiant on the world below,
Where oceans roll and rivers flow.

No sound across the welkin rung,
Save the lone notes the night-hawk sung.
Strange feelings crept o'er Allens soul,
As he pursued his evening stroll.
Alone, amid his musings grand,
In the wide world he seemed to stand.
The varied feelings of his mind,
As grave or gay, severe or kind,
So wrapped his senses in his breast
He knew not where his footsteps pressed.
He thought of Alice, high in heaven;
Of all the gifts to mortals given;

Of nobles gay, and temples grand,
He once had seen in foreign land;
Grew wroth in his true-love's defense,
And mourned her injured innocence;
Then settled down in passion kind
And stoic-like to fate resigned.

As thus in everchanging mood,
He motionless as statue stood,
A sound, as light as spirit's tread,
He faintly hears and turns his head;
Two moving forms he saw the while
Came tripping tiptoe down the isle;
'T was man and maiden he had spied,
And stooped his own tall form to hide.

A tuft of foxglove, soon behind,
Unseen he, fox-like, snug reclined,
And with foreboding dark and dread
Awaits the coming couple's tread.—

The green-eyed monster Jealousy,
Ne'er, until then, had tinged his eye,
But dark suspicion's vision keen,
Saw magnified, things else unseen,
And hatched strange vag'ries in the brain,
Which else, had in crude chaos lain.—

Close in his lair the lion laid—
On came the man, on came the maid
Hard by the foxglove's sombre shade,
And in a doubtful, flirting mood
Anear the ambush ling'ring stood.

He heard his own loved Emma's voice
In deeds of wickedness rejoice.
He saw a lustful lover's arm
Encircling her enchanting form,
And all her actions served to tell
Her wanton "steps took hold on hell."

The sight so stirred his soul to rage,
He sprang like tigress from her cage—
When her fierce bosom has been stung
By sudden stroke or loss of young—
And rushed like wrathful fiend amain,
Malignly on the guilty twain.

A flash of lightning from a cloud,
Or sudden burst of thunder loud,
Could not more fright a timid doe
Than did this charge those fiends of woe.
A keen-edged dagger, large and strong,
Was plied full fierce, and plied full long,
Until large streams from many a wound,
Fell, in *per saltum* jets around,
Upon the dark and thirsty ground.—
'T was well night's mantle formed a screen,
Or bloodier still had been the scene.—

"My son! my son!" the father cried,
"My treach'ry, and my haughty pride,
Have cost my life its purple tide!
I feel my life-blood ebbing now.
O, wipe the death sweat from my brow!

Call quick the priest! Haste, Allen, haste!
No whit of time have I to waste!"

Palsied, the arm that dealt the blow;
Quick dropped the bloody steel below.
The raging breast, so full of hell,
Now heaved a softer, gentler swell,
And tears of pity, rain-like, fell.

The pious priest, with holy tread,
Soon stood beside the dying bed.
His trembling voice, and rev'rend mien,
More solemn made the tragic scene.
He fingered back his tresses gray,
And heard the anguished layman say:
"Oh, man of God! draw nigh to me,
And ease me of my misery;
Take from my soul this heavy load,
And let me meet, in peace, my God!"

A moment's pause, when once again,
With hollow voice, the dying man
A dark confession thus began:

"Destruction's wide and beaten road,
With wicked steps I long have trod,
And deeply drained sin's flowing bowl,
Whose vitriol, like a burning coal,
Corrodes my death-deserving soul.
I 've ground the faces of the poor,
And drove the beggar from my door;
Dishonest gain and toilsome care,
Have made me now a millionaire.

I courted slander's fiendish aid,
To blast the fame of Allen's maid,
Whose angel heart, as pure as light,
Seems sinking fast beneath the blight.
'T was I, in lady's silken gown,
Who, rustling, walked the garden down,
Like maiden in her virgin pride,
A mercenary aid beside;
And feigned, as in false lover's arms,
To yield a maiden's plunder'd charms.
If ill we acted, or if well,
The tragic sequel serves to tell—

"O, memr'y blot thy fadeless scroll,
And harrow not my burning soul,
With thoughts of injured Willie Green,
On whom I tried to vent my spleen!
May I forget the turf-green sod,
Where Alice lies, a sleeping clod!
Comes o'er my soul a deathly damp!
Ah! flick'ring burns my life's dim lamp!
I feel—" Oh, Allen—Emma Glore!
A breath; a gasp; and all is o'er.

Each reader's mind can well supply
What's left untold. We pass us by
The solemn rites said o'er the bier;
The anguished friends, the mourning tear;
The will of God to mortals given,
The doom of man to hell or heaven.
'T is meet, however, that we go
Back to the tragic scene of woe,

Where we have learned that Major Brown,
Disguised as Emma, in a gown,
Was, with a dagger, stricken down.
As Allen from his crouching lair
Sprang out upon the feigning pair,
He saw a darksome, fiendish form,
Come rushing up like raging storm,
And flourish 'round his furious head
What proved a dagger, large and red.
He heard his father's fainting cries,
And struck with horror, and surprise,
He stood like one with heart of stone;
Like one with frame of wood or bone.

We need not name the secret foe,
Who struck the fatal murd'rous blow,
Or how, upon the gallows tree,
He paid, with life, the penalty;
Nor need we tell that Emma's name
From thenceforth bore a virtuous fame.
'T is deemed enough for us to say
That came the wished-for wedding day;
That in his father's palace grand,
Young Allen claimed his Emma's hand.
The happy picture we might try
To faintly sketch in passing by,
But leave to him this nobler part,
Who can do justice to the art,
And turn again to Pelew's coast,
Where late we left our hero lost.

THE MEN OF PELEW.

This dreary isle, from shore to shore,
Young Willie traversed o'er and o'er,
And found a tribe, of Adam's race,
With Christian heart, though Pagan face.
Him the good *Rupacks kindly bring
To Abba Thulle, Pelew's king;
Extending with true courtesy,
Fit treatment, due to high degree.

'T was as an angel from the skies,
Stood forth before their gazing eyes,
So great their unconcealed surprise.
They thought him some superior thing,
And bowed before him like a king.
The monarch took him by the hand,
Saying: "Welcome to our happy land!"
And bade his Rupacks, old and young,
To school him in their native tongue;
But he such rapid progress made
They deemed it vain to give him aid.
He told them of the coral grave,
Where slept his friends, the gay and brave,
Beneath the angry ocean wave.

---

*The Pelew Princes are called Rupacks. See Captain Wilson's Narrative.

And led them to the fatal shore,
To view the scene of horror o'er;
And from the wreck, which soon he spies,
His hand full many a want supplies.
The knife, the saw, the plane, the ax,
To use aright, their skill they tax.
The cannon dread, and carabine
Their curious minds could ill-divine.
Their awe terrific knew no bound,
When erst they heard their thunder-sound,
And saw the havoc they could make,
And felt their lovely island shake,
And snuffed the sulphur from the breeze;
Their hearts'-blood seemed with fear to freeze.
To them, so mighty was the spell,
All prostrate on their faces fell,
Like sons of China, at the throne,
Of their dumb gods of wood and stone,
And superstitiously adore
The manifesto of such pow'r.

Again before the king he stood,
Like monarch of superior blood,
While 'round him all the Rupacks crowd,
And in harangues, both long and loud,
They labored hard, as Raphael, each,
To paint the scene upon the beach;
And Fancy's glowing pencil drew
Exaggerative, over-true,
The picture, insomuch the crown
From Abba Thulle's head fell down;

While his majestic, regal form
Rocked like a vessel in a storm,
And pale as statue made of stone,
He beckoned Willie to the throne,
And bade him wear the prostrate crown,
And on the kingly seat sit down,
The while exclaiming: "This must be
The work of some divinity!"

But Willie bowing, smiling said:
"Thy crown remain upon thy head;
Thyself upon the throne; though first
Come, view the things but now rehearsed,
And read in them the coming fall
Of thy worst foe, proud Artingall."

The king-automaton obeyed,
While, o'er his brow, alternate played
Fear, hope, and doubt in strong array,
Each striving which should win the day;
But when, before him, was displayed,
The grandeur of the cannonade,
Lit up his face a smile; his eye
Was fire; his heart beat wildly high;
And dreams of glory seemed to throng
His brain; each crowding each along.
And ere another week was flown,
His warriors all stood round the throne,
And heard the royal voice proclaim
Our hero's unpretending fame,

And give him absolute command
Of all the forces in the land;
When all agree, as voice of one,
That Willie be the king's first son.

Now, Pelew's shore had oft been trod
By Artingall's fierce sons of blood,
Who sallied forth, with spear and bow,
To lay their warlike neighbors low;
And scarce lived there, on Pelew's coast,
A warrior brave, who could not boast
Of some great deed, or show a scar
In honor of some recent war;
Or having bathed the neighb'ring strand
With blood of foe drawn by his hand;
And so well-matched the kingdoms were
That neither long the palm could bear:
Mayhap to-day would Pelew lead;
To-morrow Artingall succeed:
But Willie's arms and native skill,
With confidence his forces fill,
And wildly Thulle's pulses thrill;
While dreams of conquest flit him by
Athwart the vault of hope's bright sky;
And all the island near and far,
To learn the art of Christian war,
Flock daily 'round, the ranks to fill
And catch their master's martial skill;
For rumor's tongue had lately said,
That Artingall, all on parade,

Was marshaling her thousands strong
Tow'rd Pelew's isles intent along.

No tearful eye, nor smiting knee,
Nor trembling form showed wish to flee;
The news was hailed with shouts of joy,
From gray-haired sire to beardless boy;
And Thulle's Rupacks longed again,
To meet in arms, the coming train;
And make amends for battle lost
When last they fought upon the coast.

SUPERSTITION.

The king of day, with stately tread,
Was seeking his nocturnal bed.
The warbling songsters in the groves
Were pouring out their happy loves.
The orange and the lemon shed
Their dulcet fragrance o'er the head;
Whilst falling dews and waving trees,
Lent, each, refreshings to the breeze.

Then came soft evening in the west,
With twilight's scarf upon her breast,
And high her spangled flag unfurled,
Wide o'er an oriental world.
Such eves as this inspire the mind
With thoughts of supernat'ral kind.

The work of training for the day
Was o'er; the idle troopers lay
In circling squads, the palms beneath,
Or wandered o'er the neighboring heath.
Oppressed and weary on the ground
Those fast in slumber's chains were bound,
Or whiled the tardy moments by
With tales of fancy wrought full high.

Love talked of beauty's tender heart;
Ambition took a warlike part;
8

And superstition's person gray
Descanted much on ghost and fay;
The Rupack lords of nobler blood,
Anear the royal presence stood
Discussing now the arts of war;
Comparing these with those afar.

Now, in promiscuous, even tide,
The conversation seemed to glide
Not like the moments, dull and slow,
But swift as thought's electric flow.
So much delight the tales they hear,
As pour they in upon the ear,
Each feels a charm himself come o'er,
He mayhap never felt before;
Each quizzing each the while to learn,
The thoughts that in the others burn,
And from the whole, young Willie brings
To light their faith in men and things.

They say the diamond stars aboon
Are children of the silver moon;
That Luna wed the dazzling sun
Ten thousand years ere time begun;
That Sol created life and light,
And filled the earth with beauty bright;
Gives good men homes high in the sky,
When clod-like in the earth they lie.
But ties the wicked down to earth,
And curses them with endless birth;
Where ghosts and wizards here, for aye,
They, sorrowing discontented stay,

In forest dark, and dismal den,
And haunt the sinful sons of men.

They told him of a gloomy thing:
Lee Boo, a brother of the king,
A Rupack of illustrious name,
And warrior of undying fame,
A tale thus told in Willie's ear,
That gave him strange delight to hear.

LEE BOO'S TALE.

"There is, in wicked Artingall,
  A high, stupendous waterfall,
  Whose thund'ring water constantly
  Leaps from a mount above the sky,
  And pours its foaming self along
  In rushing, roaring, angry song.

"The woods and hills stand trembling round
  For very fear; so mad the sound;
  And ev'ry day, if clear the sky,
  When Sol comes forth, rejoicing high,
  A fiery bow, half bent is seen,
  All painted red, and blue, and green,
  From which oft blazing arrows fly,
  And shoot beyond the vaulted sky;
  Or strike, perchance, some fleecy cloud,
  Or bathe the moon's sweet face with blood.

"Unnumb'red milk-white wizards play
  Amid its waters, day by day,
  And dance to music soft and sweet,
  Which human tongue can not repeat;
  And bathe themselves, its waters in,
  To wash away their deeds of sin;
  And should a trav'ler pass them by,
  They spread their wings and at him fly.

Hard by where these ill monsters lave,
There stands, wide-mouthed, a yawning cave,
With steps descending, dark and steep,
Down into rooms profoundly deep,
Where, nightly, fays their vigils keep.
When last I fought on foreign strand,
I halted near this wizard land,
And listed softest music's swell
As sweet it rose, and gently fell,
Like evening dew upon the ear;
Then, more enchanting, loud and clear,
An answer came from hill and dale.
Chill ran my blood! I felt a quail
Rush o'er my frame much like the dread
Of youth, when first to battle led.

"In ev'ry tree there seemed a tongue;
  A song in ev'ry bush; there rung
  Such sweet, unearthly sounds. I felt
  As though my throbbing heart would melt.
  I wished myself far from the dell,
  And labored hard to break the spell;
  For 'round my person, bleaching, lay
  Fresh human bones, the work of fay;
  I found the sweetness of the song
  Was but to lure me still along,
  And when we once have reached the cave
  No arm, on earth, has pow'r to save.

"I met the foe in dread array,
  And bravely fought, but lost the day;

Nor wonder why, for who could fight
'Gainst human foe and wizard might?
And should you meet, anear this cave,
With all your guns and warriors brave,
Half Artingall in war array,
You, too, methinks, would lose the day:
Once more upon the wizard strand
I would not stop for all the land.
I would not see the spot again
For Abba Thulle's whole domain.

'And should the foe before you flee,
In that vile land beyond the sea,
O, go not near the mystic cave,
I charge you by the ocean's wave!
I charge you by yon blazing sun!
By all the stars that round him run!
And by the moon, the sun's bright queen!
By all things else that eye hath seen!
I charge you! Shun that place as death,
Or down the earth you sink beneath!"—

The camp is still—its thousands rest
Like conscience in the honest breast:
The moon, upon her fourteenth night,
Bedecked with robes of softest light,
Is riding now her highest height.
No zephyr sports among the trees,
No brooklet murmurs melodies.
Upon the lake no wavelet plays;
No roaring notes from ocean's bass.

No moving thing; no stir, no sound
To break the silence deep, profound;
Save when some sleeper's aching side
Bids him a softer bed provide;
Or when the wild-cock's clarion shrill,
Comes echoing from the distant hill.
Such eves enwrap the sluggish brain
With slumber's thickest counterpane;
But pensive minds the barrier break;
The very stillness makes them wake.
This Willie's lot; in mental pain
He courted slumber's aid in vain.

Lashed by the furies of the mind,
A moment's rest he could not find.
Long trains of thought, with heavy tread,
Came rushing through his aching head.
Now imagery, in dazzling blaze,
Brings up the ghost of other days;
Oft shifts the glimm'ring, fitful scene,
From grave to gay, wild to serene.
Now musing on the tales of fay,
As tossing on his bed he lay,
He smiled to think this simple race
Could for such vagaries find a place;
But charity, with mantle wide,
Steps forth, their heathen thoughts to hide;
And pity drowns his smiles; and now
Sad reminiscence crowds his brow.

In thought's vast field, his Christian land
In gloomy glory seems to stand,

Where Superstition—awful god—
E'en there still rules with iron rod.
The tales he heard, when yet a boy—
That withered oft his childish joy,
And made him still the closer cling
To mother's 'fending apron string—
An overwhelming offset plead
In favor of this simpler breed.
Unable to destroy the spell
He rose and sought the dewy dell,
A silent promenade to take,
Where danced the moonbeams on the lake,
And snuff the soft and balmy air
And thus dispel his haunting care.

THE BATTLE.

But hark! what's that now greets the ear,
Like stealthy footsteps drawing near?
Say, heard ye not that trembling tread,
Come like far thunder o'er the head?
No! 'T was hallucination's child!
'T was but some brain-born fancy wild.
But hush! hist! from the shady plane,
Methinks it rides the air again!

"They come! they come! I hear the tramp!"
A voice cries out within the camp—
"The foe! the foe! he comes! he comes!
Now for your country and your homes!"
Shouts Prince Lee Boo so fierce and clear
Ten thousand sleepers spring to spear.
Ten thousand stalwart warriors stood,
With ax and bow to shed the blood
Of Artingall; and braver band
Ne'er faced a foe in any land—
"To arms! to arms!" bold Willie cries,
The cannon booms—the foe—he flies
Like lightning from an angry cloud—
Alarmed to hear such thunder loud—
Or skims like deer o'er hill and brake,
Nor stops for fen or miry lake,
But coastward fast their way they take;

The rills and brooklets heedless leap,
As madly on their course they sweep,
Nor stop to turn their faces back,
For fear the foe is on their track.

Behind the eager campers yell,
Like hunter's hounds, or fiends of hell—
The wild confusion of the chase
Rebounding echo promptly pays—
In vain do Willie and Lee Boo
Cry: "Fall in line and them pursue!"
Regardless quite of martial line,
With bow, and spear, and carabine,
They bound like lions to the coast—
For each now deemed himself a host.

When gray-eyed morn peeped o'er the lea
It saw the foe far out at sea,
And Willie, with his anxious host
In hot pursuit upon the coast.
That morning rose the king of day,
Not clothed in glory's brilliant ray,
But with a red and blood-shot eye,
He rolled him up the eastern sky,
And seemed a red-hot ball of fire;
Or some great god in dreadful ire,
And gazed upon the world below,
As bent upon its overthrow;
So angry did his face appear,
The gentle moon seemed struck with fear.

She bade, anon the world adieu,
And hastened from her throne of blue,
And diffident as blushing bride,
She trembling sank upon the tide.

With bustling steps and rattling din,
The Pelews jump their pirogues in,
Their ten foot spears wave over head,
Like reeds in wind of winter dead.
Each warrior grasps a well-tried bow,
That reaches quite from head to toe,
And from each back full quivers swing,
Well feathered from the wild-cock's wing;
While to each dark and sunburnt side
A huge, rude battle ax is tied.

The leaders of the murd'rous fleet,
Equipped with musketry complete,
Fast fly before the driving wind;
As rapidly the braves behind.
Five hundred p'rogues, at their best,
With rising prow, and all abreast,
Skim o'er the ocean's rolling crest,
As lightly as an English sail,
Or feathers in a driving gale.
The flying oars 'mid waters sport,
Like finny shoal of monstrous sort,
And back upon the rocky shore
The oar-beat waves, rebounding roar.

On fly "pursuers; on pursued;"
Each in an anxious, hurried mood;

The first in quest of fight and blood;
The last through superstitious dread,
Has homeward turned his flying head.
'T is not the fear of Pelew's host,
Makes Arra Tushee seek his coast;
For well he knows his brawny band
In brav'ry vies with any land.
Full well he knows, when last they fought,
A vict'ry grand he lightly bought;
It is the cannon's awful roar
That drives him to his native shore.

The splashing oars and vocal hum,
To Artingall still nearer come.
Pursuers and pursued anon,
Come swan-like, swiftly sailing on.
Now Arra Tushee strikes the shore;
His host, like locusts, on it pour.
Each throbbing heart beats wondrous high,
With true returning bravery—
For who could see his native land,
Invaded by a foreign band,
And feel no patriotic fire
His bosom burn, his soul inspire?
The recreant wretch, "if such there be,"
That such a sight, unmoved could see,
Deserves no country, kindred, friend,
Its fruits to give, their joys to lend.
Unhonored let the living dead,
Oblivion's path unnoticed tread;

Unhonored live, unhonored die;
Uncoffined let him tombless lie;
No friendly aid or watchful care;
Or stone to plead remembrance there,
Or tell that such a wretch had birth,
Or with his being cursed the earth;
E'en the poor bee, in her rude home
Yields but with life, her precious comb.—

"Arm! Arm! ye sons of Artingall!"
Cries Arra Tushee, "one and all!"
From mouth to mouth the word was given,
And 'plauding shouts rent high the heaven.
From plain to mountain went the sound;
From plain to mountain, 'round and 'round;
And echo loud from mount to plain,
Brings swiftly back the same again.
The fighting minions, near and far,
Fill rapidly the ranks of war.

In high commanding, savage tone,
King Tushee bade his troops lead on,
And halt anear the wizard cave,
And meet the coming Pelew knave,
With spear, and club, and trusty knife,
Nor yield the battle but with life—
Slow wind they on o'er vale and hill,
Like lazy herd at evening still,
Then through the wood the dark ranks filed,
Like Indians in a western wild;
Then spread the long meand'ring train
Upon a wide extended plain,

Where halts brave Tushee with his men,
Hard by the yawning, mystic den,
And takes a strong, defensive stand,
And waits the coming Pelew band.
Down on their knees they humbly fall,
And faithfully and loudly call
Upon the sprites within the cave;
Invoking them from foe to save,
As did they when before they stood
Upon that same red field of blood.

In answer to their fervent prayer,
The fancied music fills the air.*
They see the songsters in the groves
Have ceased to measure out their loves;
And flock in circling droves around,
To catch the flowing dulcet sound.
And from the pebbly streamlets clear,
The sporting fish leap up to hear;
Each moving thing on hill and plain,
Enchanted, stops to catch the strain.
Encouraged by such mighty spell,
Each bosom quickly heaved and fell,
And firm to foot each warrior springs;
His dangling war club lat'ral swings.

His left hand grasps with purpose fell,
A knife, made from the muscle shell.
The right fast waves a spear on high
And martial flames light up each eye,

---

*See page 116, and read Lee Boo's description of this Cave.

All wait the foe impatiently—
Like prowling wolves, small distance back,
The yelling Pelew's sought the track.
They scoured the wood and scanned the plain,
And madly wound the hills in vain.
But Willie, with undaunted breast,
Gave little time for halt or rest.
He bade, anon, his aid, Lee Boo,
First down the vale the foe pursue;
And hand to hand with forces all,
To win the day, or bravely fall.
Himself, with well charged musketry,
Intently wound across the lea,
And, with a corps of fifty men,
Marched straight unto the wizard den.

Obedient to the high bequest,
This stream of ire hard onward pressed,
Where lofty trees their shadows flung,
Like giants tall, when time was young.
So deep that vale, its hills between,
That scarce the day-god's rays were seen;
While stood the tow'ring mounts so high,
Their summits almost prop the sky.
As dang'rous seemed this pass to be,
As Greece's famed Thermopylæ;
Yet on, so great their thirst for blood,—
Like rivers swelled by recent flood—
The warrior current, rushing, boiled,
Nor scarce from mountain's foot recoiled.

At length they reached the battle plain,
Anon Lee Boo prepared his train.

From tow'rd the wizard waterfall
Came meeting them, fierce Artingall.
The armies circle round and round,
Each striving hard for choice of ground;
And clearer each can hear the hum
Of other, as they closer come;
Still nearer, yet, with lance on high;
With face to face, and eye to eye,
And foot to foot and hand to hand,
The armies now a moment stand;
Then, like the rending earthquake's shock
The rushing onset madly broke.

The noise rolled o'er the far-off plain,
Like distant hail or roaring rain;
But to the more adjacent ear,
'T was dying groan and splint'ring spear;
And bang and clang of ax and bow,
And cuffing sound of stunning blow.
Like forest dead, when rocked by wind;
The spears wave high before, behind.
Far up the feath'ry fragments fly,
Like oceans' milky foam on high,
When lash their waves the stormy sky.
So harsh the martial rattle pealed,
'T was like the crash of *Flodden Field;*
Or *Linden's* boiling sea of ire,
When raging like a world on fire.

Young Willie reached the wizard den,
But saw nor foe nor Pelew men;
But heard the clash of ax and spear,
And said, "destruction must be near."
He scaled, anon, the nearest hill;
A moment stood, aghast and still,
And viewed the scene that met his sight,
Like Bonaparte, from Tabor's height,
When Kleber, with his men below,
Made Turkish blood like rivers flow.
Alternate flee both foe and friend,
Then rally, charge, again contend,
And mix in wild and mad turmoil,
Like mighty maelstrom's aqueous boil;
Or wind-beat waves, now high, now low,
They rise and fall, and ebb and flow;
Now face to face, and hand to hand,
Lee Boo and Tushee struggling stand.

They whirl, they surge, they bend, they reel,
And strain each nerve from head to heel;
A moment more they panting lie;
The first below, the last on high;
But sudden flounce and rising strain,
Bring, quickly, both to foot again;
When fast and hard their lances ply,
And crimson streamlets spouting fly,
And swiftly fall in jets around,
And paint with red the grass and ground.

9

At last, Lee Boo, like giant oak,
When felled by woodman's final stroke,
Fell, waving high his broken spear,
His panic-stricken troops to cheer—
No highland chief on Scottish shore,
In chivalry's best days of yore,
E'er better wielded broad claymore,
In single fight or famous wars,
Than did these heathen sons of Mars—

Up rose a shout, so fierce and high,
That Pelew's awe-struck warriors fly,
Like chaff before a whirling wind,
And fast pursue the foe behind.
Like flocks of birds, their arrows dart,
And ranks of Pelews 'neath the smart,
Besmeared with wounds and dyed with gore,
Fall, welt'ring, down to rise no more.

Brave Willie but one moment stood
To gaze upon this scene of blood;
Then bade *his* men the foe pursue,
And down the hill, like lightning, flew.
They reached the field; their musketry,
Like thunder, boomed o'er hill and lea.
Up sprang Lee Boo, who lay as dead,
And waved his spear around his head,
And "Rally! Rally!" was the cry—
To rank the scatt'red Pelews hie.

Deep in the pass the parties stand
With rocky walls on either hand;

Lee Boo behind and Green before,
Hot lead and arrows hail-like pour,
Upon the foe that stands between,
A prey to Mars in Death's ravine.
Dread panic seized King Tushee's band,
And stiff with fear they doubting stand.
They look to left; they look to right;
And view aloft the scaleless height;
They look before, and look behind,
But lead and arrows only find.
Cut off from ev'ry chance of flight,
More deadly still becomes the fight.
Grown desp'rate now, in stern despair,
Like lion roused from sleeping lair,
Mad Tushee's eye, with flashes shone,—
"Follow," he cried, and rushed him on;
But so unequal now the fray,
That Artingall soon lost the day,
And with it, too—O, sad to tell!
Her mighty chief, King Tushee, fell.
And lay beneath the victor's pow'r,
A ruined and demolished tow'r.
And so impregnable the pass,
Death mows the conquered down like grass.
Behind, high ramparts of the dead,
Pelew still plies her weapons dread.

The vanquished see their leader die,
And loud, and louder, "quarters" cry;
But true to Nature's savage will,
On, madly slay the victors still,

Despite the loud behest of Green,
Whose heart bled o'er the brutish scene;
But on a sight so sad to all,
Here quickly let the curtain fall.
'T were sad to tell, in measured lay,
The woes of that eventful day.
'T is quite enough, methinks, to tell,
Three thousand vanquished warriors fell,
And found a grave in the Wizard Dell,
And for the glory of that day,
A thousand braves the Pelews pay—
A victor's gain, to count the cost,
Is oft as bad as a battle lost.
Why should the blood of thousands run
To satisfy the whims of one?
Blood, too, as rich, as dear, as red,
Perhaps, as courses kingly head.
God speed the time may reach earth's shore,
When nations shall learn war no more!
When the spear, instead, shall prune the tree,
And blood red fruit its trophies be;
When the sword shall thrust the tardy soil,
And Earth shall yield, in peace, her spoil;
Unharming and unharmed shall dwell
The lamb and lion in one cell;
And peacefully together lie,
Beneath a soft millennial sky,
The leopard and the kid; and men
Return to Eden's land again.

When passed the din of battle by,
Returned again a peaceful sky.

Our hero viewed the gory ground,
Where friend and foe lay heaped around,
And, as the slipp'ry field he roved,
His noble soul with pity moved.
He thought of Honor and its laws,
Of Honor's deeds, in Honor's cause,
Of thousands who, in dea lly strife,
For honor's crown paid lands and life;
Till into speech his musings broke,
And thus his lips as follows spoke:
"O, soul! come be thyself again!
And henceforth from man's blood abstain!
Rivers of human blood have flown
To gild with fame one hero's crown!
What millions fell in Persian State
That Alexander might be great?
Brave Cæsar's laurels owe their red
To seas of gore by Romans shed;
And Bonaparte no glory wears
Save that bestowed by bloody Mars,
If this be glory, may disgrace
Forever clothe my humble face!"—

Again the Pelews home return;
With glory their proud bosoms burn.
The heroes stand before the throne
And make our hero's glory known,
And for the brav'ry he displayed,
Is ruler of the conquered made.
Fit ceremonies duly said,
Attest the mem'ry of the dead.

The common warrior's bravery
Is sung before high royalty;
And feast, and mirth, and praise, the while
Show their repute throughout the isle.
Now with a true and well-tried band
Prince Green returns to Tushee's land,
Where all the tribes of Artingall
Before him in submission fall.

Anon, howe'er, so mild his sway,
Their fears, like frost-work, pass away;
And into warm affection run,
Like snow beneath a cheering sun;
And soon his gentle, firm command
Was stronger than the tyrant's wand—
To iron despots who would rule,
By laws laid down in bigot school,
This fact, methinks, should go to prove
That cruelty must yield to love;
But whether true or false this be
We leave to deep philosophy,
And haste to tell in manner grave
Our hero's visit to the cave,
Which Prince Lee Boo's creative mind
Had filled with sprites of ev'ry kind;
Indeed young Willie heard the swell
Of music soft in that lone dell,
Contrasting with the war-notes pealed
The day he won the battle-field;
What wonder then that he should feel
Desire the myst'ry to unseal.

THE WIZARD CAVE.

Short time he passed since first he came
To govern in King Thulle's name,
Ere he, with guides and armed men,
Sat out to view the Wizard Den.
The dappled wing of morn had spread
Its rising glories o'er his head,
As if, with visage mild and gray,
To harbinger the new-born day.
The day king next himself uprose
Unnumbered beauties to disclose.
His spangled beard in spangled rays
He lent, anon, to nature's face,
And roused again the sleeping earth
To smiles of joy and songs of mirth.
The pearly dew from out its eyes
Looked forth ten thousand rainbow dyes;
Each spear, and blade, and shrub of green,
Dressed in its richest robes was seen;
Each purple pink and ruddy rose
Made incense for the day god's nose;
Each sylvan songster tuned its throat
And piped its ever-changing note.
All nature, with poetic taste,
Praised Sol in language pure and chaste;
More beauteous morn ne'er put to flight
The leaden shades of sable night.

Young Willie viewed these glories spread
Around, above, beneath his head,
With rapture and delight; and thought
Of pictures heathen fancy wrought;
And felt how man's untutored mind
A very god in Sol could find;
And felt how man's untutored sense,
Could image Sol's omnipotence:
Thought followed thought, in varied mood,
Until before the cave he stood,
Where all the grandeur of the land
Seemed there to center; there to stand,
Like rays converged by convex lens;
A roaring waterfall descends,
Crowned with his seven-colored bow.
There, mounts so high and vales so low;
There lakes, and rills, and woodlawn plains,
Were picturing to his classic brains
A world of beauty; but the thought
Of wizards in the cave soon brought
Him to the grotto's mouth, despite
His love of scenery; and a light
Was quickly struck when all the band
Down ventured to that nether land.

Their torch, sun-like, lit up this world
And untold beauties there unfurled.
The marble walls, of snowy white,
Reflected back this torchy light,
Resembling, in their grandeur tall,
The splendor of some princely hall.

High from the ceiling, chandeliers
Hung, as designed for noble peers;
But far before, the view was bound
Hard by a field of darkness round;
Yet, as they journeyed, fast it fled
Like Night before the Morning's tread,
And left behind, to plainer view,
Fresh beauties; ever changing; new.

At length the party stood before
A wide and massive open door,
Yet entered not, for there they spied
A giant huge, of monstrous stride,
Whose head did prop the ceiling high,
As mountains seem to prop the sky;
And seemed to stand as sentinel
To guard from harm the inner dell;
While winged fays, both large and small,
Thick-made and slender, low and tall;
Of ev'ry shape and mien, stood 'round
Like soldiers on a battle ground.

The awe-struck natives prostrate fell,
And prayed the genii of the dell
Their lives to spare; but such a sight
Our hero filled with rich delight.
Instead of giants, fierce and tall,
He saw a large baronial hall
With columns chaste, on either side,
As if by artist's hand supplied;
And stalactites and chandeliers
He saw, and fain would quell the fears

Of those who trembling, doubting, stood
In this deep home of solitude.
While he with pleasure, these with pain,
Viewed o'er and o'er the scene again,
There rose a soft and dulcet strain
Of lute or harp. A mighty spell
Upon the natives instant fell,
And Green himself as statue still
Stood long and felt his pulses thrill
With holy awe; nor wished to move,
For that sweet song discoursed of love,
In soft, familiar, plaintive strain,
Like that oft heard across the main,
But which he ne'er should hear again.

Why stands he thus, pale as with fear?
Why bathes his eye the flowing tear?
Why has his hand the bright torch lower'd?
Why sinks his frame, as if o'erpower'd?
His mouth why thus agape; his ear
Why strained as if his doom to hear?
Does he suppose he there shall meet
The spirit form of Alice sweet?
Ah, vain and foolish thought! then why
Does he seem half disposed to fly?
Has mystery so much of pow'r
That it can lock bold reason's tow'r,
And with its same strange, magic key
Make bankrupt all his bravery?

No! the sweet music of the strain
Came, bringing loves and home again,

And maids of beauty; train on train.
His former youth before him rose
Bedecked with joy; devoid of woes,
And, like a lovely angel, passed
Upon the wings of that sweet blast.
Those dulcet sounds, so passing fair,
Were struck to Willie's fav'rite air.

With mighty impulse thus inspired,
And heaving bosom strangely fired,
He left his comrades in the rear
And forward moved, despite their fear,
Until he passed the massive door,
When clearer, louder than before,
He heard the music; and a voice
That made his inmost soul rejoice.

A moment now he stops to hear
Those silver tones that strike so clear,
Like welcome news, his list'ning ear.
Now hurries on, with flying feet,
The nymph or naiad form to greet,
Till, at the grotto's farthest side,
A beauteous maid at length he spied,
Reclining on a couch of green,
With harp in hand of silver sheen.
Politely to the form he bowed;
At a respectful distance stood;
With wave of hand and courteous smile,
He queried thus in modest style:

"O! beauteous thing of earth or heaven!
Nymph! Naiad! Angel! Ghost unshriven!

Whate'er thyself, whate'er thy birth,
On land, or sea; in sky, or earth;
I pray thee quickly tell; and chase
The mighty mystery from this place.
Of form divine, and angel voice,
And harp of true celestial choice,
Why dwell'st within this cavern drear?
When thou couldst thrill a nation's ear;
Or do those echoing walls around,
Stamp sweetness on the wings of sound?
Or, am I lab'ring 'neath the spell
Of some foul fiend of nether hell?
Come, tell me, if thou canst, the why
Thy strain brought tear-drops to mine eye.

"Mayhap thou 'st braved the stormy main, ·
To shun a world of woe and pain.
Hast ever heard, or ever seen,
Columbia's strand, or Willie Green?"

Anon she left her humble bed;
Her auburn ringlets back she spread
In flowing curls behind her head.
Upon the ground her harp she threw,
And, thought-like, to the speaker flew,
And shrieked, and on his bosom fell
Crying, "Haste, dear Willie, haste, and tell
How came you to this dismal dell?"
Locked in each other's arms they stood:
"Alice!" he cried.   A mighty flood
Of feeling, like a flowing sea,
O'erwhelmed the tongue and drowned the eye,

And silence, king-like, seized again
His crown, and recommenced his reign.

No vulgar eye, nor prying ear,
Could hear the sigh, nor see the tear,
Nor share the joy, the rapt'rous twain,
Felt in each other's arms again;
Nor less the bliss, nor quicker by,
Because no stranger face was nigh.

"Alice!" he cried, in joyous glee,
"But for thy touching minstrelsy
I ne'er had seen thy sweet face more,
This side of heaven's delightful shore!
Haste now! thy fairy acts explain,
And thus relieve my puzzled brain?"

"My life! my love!" she cried,
"I 'll tell thee all, whate'er betide.
A coward from my face you fled,
As from some danger fierce and dread,
Not daring me again to see,
Because you'd graced the gallows tree.
And for my brother's absent head,
Had well nigh hanged till 'dead, dead, dead!'
How light you valued my poor love,
Your flight from me must go to prove.
Report's long tongue soon said to me
'He's fled across the briny sea,
Where far Australia's golden strand
Invites him to her sunny land.'

I shut my heart against my home
And tender ties of youth, to roam
Across a wide and angry sea
In search, my love, in search of thee.

"But when far out upon the main
He heaved his breast as if in pain
And drifted us to this vile shore
Whence I had feared I'd 'scape no more.
Our gallant ship, the 'Ocean Belle,'
Was swallowed by the angry swell
Of wind-beat waves, and all save me
Now sleep in peace beneath the sea.

"A floating fragment, like a friend,
Arose and bore me to this land.
My bread I borrowed from the tree;
My meat's the oyster from the sea,
This humble couch, before us spread,
Of downy grass, I make my bed.
The harp you gave, my only joy
Since here I came, gives me employ,
And chases from my home away
All natives that may near me stray.

"They seem to think my minstrelsy,
Is made by monsters of the sea,
And from it, as from death they flee,
And leave the cave to peace and me.
For three long years this living grave
Has held me like a hapless slave.

But I have found mixed in its sand
Rich pearls that vie with any land;
And diamonds of a purer kind,
Than on Brazilian shores we find.
Though but the slave of stern despair,
I boast myself a millionaire;
And should we ever dwell again,
On sweet Ohio's fertile plain,
The wealth that we shall then possess
Shall all our friends and neighbors bless.

"But, ah! my love, how can we flee,
From this wild shore back o'er the sea?
And must we stay forever more,
From fair Columbia's dulcet shore?
O, can we hope to live again
With friends and parents over the main?

"Hark, Willie! hear that savage call,
Wild echoing o'er this Hadean hall!
It is, my love, it is I fear
Some savage native hov'ring near,
For which we both may pay full dear."—
She lifts her harp, and from its strings
Unearthly cadence sweetly springs.—
"'T is thus these superstitious men,"
She said, "I drive from this lone den,
Whene'er a straggler comes anear,
Or I could have no peace I fear."—
Adown her harp she lays again—
The walls take up the sweet refrain—

" And ne'er has failed this harp to save,
Me from intrusion in this cave;
For none e'er dared until your call
To 'face the music' in this hall.
But had a savage foe pursued
Me in this nether solitude,
He should have found me far below,
Where Stygian waters deadly flow,
And where have I long since prepared
A strong trap-door—a sure reward—
A door that quickly would have hurled
All enemies to Pluto's world;
But Willie, pray come, give to me
The past four years of history:
Pray fill the blank that now you find
Upon the tablet of my mind."

Now Alice hears, with anxious ear,
The tale of hope, and love, and fear;
Of Allen Brown and Emma Glore;
How Willie sailed the o can o'er;
Of all his wealth and honor's won;
Of his career at Washington;
Of the cold corpse, with auburn hair,
Stiff lying in its icy lair;
Of the sad news of Mrs. Brown,
And the Major, too, in his silken gown;
Of the strange tale, of Prince Lee Boo,
So tinged with fancy through and through;
Of breathing thought, and burning word;
Of all that Alice had not heard.

Upon her face, now grave now gay,
Her tears and smiles, alternate, play
Like rain and sun in fickle May.
And said she then, " If pass we o'er
A western rout, a western door,
Will open to the rocky shore,
Where ocean's breaking waters foam,
And where I entered first this home."
They pass them on; she leads the way;
His brilliant torch reveals the gray;
The white; the changing wall;
As wander they from hall to hall;
Now glitters here a mimic spire;
There giants throw reflected fire,
And stalactites of ev'ry dye,
And shape, and look, fast fix the eye
On those grand ceilings, hung so high.

And when they came to Pluto's pit,
The trap-door sprang from over it;
When down a stone our hero hurled
Into that bottomless wat'ry world,
Ten thousand, thousand, thousand feet,
Where Echo failed her to repeat.

At length they reach the grotto's mouth,
They northward look, and look to south;
Then throw the eye against the west,
Where the pillars of heaven on the ocean rest,
And long drink in this grand, sublime,
Like gazers from some starry clime.

10

They spy, at length, a tiny sail,
Like a white swan, before the gale,
And hope and fear alternate rise,
Like sun and cloud before the skies;
And high their throbbing bosoms bound,
As fancy's thoughts come dancing round,
And bringing back fond mem'ry o'er,
Their long lost home; their native shore;
And driving fear's foreboding form
As dead leaves drive before a storm.
The plowing prow soon points to shore;
They feel their troubles all are o'er.
Their diamonds now they quickly pack,
When lo! the vessel takes a "tack!"
And leaves dead hope on palsied wing
Her own sad requiem to sing.
But look again! she steers once more,
Directly for the rock-ribbed shore,
When hope, more bounding than before,
On wings ecstatic seems to rise
And circling, sweep the upper skies.

The "*Sea Bird*" nears them; now they hail
And get an answer from the sail;
And when the vessel tips the shore
Their souls with joy seem running o'er.
They, kneeling, humbly thank the Lord
And quickly find themselves aboard.

Their vessel touches classic Rome
Before its final reach for home.

We lengthen not our verse to tell
The many things which there befell;
As how our lovers toured the place
In search of ev'ry classic grace;
How Coliseum sits sublime
A crown upon the head of Time,
And how huge crumbling heaps lie furled
Where Cæsar's rod once quaked the world,
And piles of palace ruins say:
"Like us their power hath passed away."

And from these sights our travl'rs draw
Another proof of God's great law
That Hist'ry's ever busy pen
Writes down of nation's, as of men,
The birth and death, the rise and fall,
On ruined tower and crumbling hall;
Aye! shows us how they come and go,
E'en as the flick'ring fire-fly's glow.

Tread where they will, those ruins, dead,
Display the Art of ages fled;
Here some true Angeloan hand
Has strewn its beauties o'er the land;
And there, a Raphael's gift displays
The glory of those elder days.

But quit they soon this classic strand,
And hie them to their native land,
Where friends, with bursting hearts, rejoice;
Where music tunes its mellow voice;

Where the tables groan with dainty cheer,
And the laugh of mirth rings loud and clear;
And miles on miles the cry goes round,
"*The dead yet lives; the lost is found!*"

But never yet hath been revealed,
What mystery hath so long concealed,
The name or place of her, whose form
Was buried by the wint'ry storm.
But which now sleeps, with its eyes of lead,
In the marble city of the dead
With the name of "*Alice*" above its head;
And which will sleep 'neath the turfy sod
Till waked by the voice of the living God.

But why prolong our simple verse
Or strive in closing to rehearse
The many things, or large or small,
Which then transpired at "*Eden Hall,*"
Enough it is to say, in sooth,
Thenceforth the course of love "ran smooth,"
Smooth as the meadow's gentle rill
When storms are hushed and meadows still;
Enough it is for us to say
That came at last the wedding day.
And with it, all the joys of life
As realized by man and wife.
For wedded "love has dearer names.
And firmer ties, and sweeter claims,

Than e'er unwedded hearts can feel,
Than wedded hearts can e'er reveal;
Pure as the charities above
Rise the sweet sympathies of love;
And closer cords than those of life
Unite the husband to the wife."

Enough it is for us to tell
That Providence doth all things well;
That man may oft "devise his way,"
But God his steps directs for aye.

FINIS

ERRATA.

Page 24, line 7 from top, read *o'er her*, not "o'er silken."

Page 30, line 4 from bottom, first word read *Resides*, not "Besides."

Page 66, line 10 from top, sixth word, read *Allen* not "Willie."

Page 74, line 4 from top, fourth word, read *boundless* not "bounless."

Page 74, line 10 from top, first word, read *For* not "The."

Page 74, line 8 from bottom, third word, read *omnific* not "omnipotent."

Page 86, line 4 from top, second word, read *lets* not "let."

Page 98, line 1 from top, first word, read *How* not "Now."

Page 128, line 5 from bottom, third word, read *the* not "their."

Page 132, line 3 from bottom, fourth word, read *laws* not "land."

Page 136, line 13 from bottom, sixth word, read *woodland* not "woodlawn."

Page 143, line 14 from bottom, fifth word, read *o'er* not "over."

Page 148, line 7 from bottom, sixth word, read *Nature* not "meadows."

www.ingramcontent.com/pod-product-compliance
Lightning Source LLC
Chambersburg PA
CBHW030905050726
47500CB00009B/1037